One Day Things Changed:

Fictional Short Stories of
Love, Betrayal, and Redemption

Katrina A. McCain

Poet Katrina McCain
PO Box 5211
Greensboro, NC 27435

Cover & Design Layout:
Carlos V. Kaigler /C'vaughn'K Graphic Designs/ The Poet B.GKL

Proofreader:
Author The Poet B.GKL

ISBN: 978-1-7379392-1-4

One Day Things Changed

Fictional Short Stories of
Love, Betrayal, and Redemption

Dedication

This book is dedicated to the best parts of me...

Arrius Lavey McCain
&
Angela LeAnn McCain

Table of Contents

Foreword

It is in our human nature to find success in comfortability and familiarity. It is only when we step outside of our comfort zone do we reach our fullest potential. Within this new book, Poet Katrina McCain has done just that. As you indulge in the word play over the next 140 pages, Poet Katrina McCain will take you on a journey through the depths of her creative spaces.

From expressing the boundless impact of love to addressing current events, McCain has produced two exceptional forms of work. However, she has taken a monumental shift in format and content. McCain pours her entire being into short stories with underlying messages and concepts, which are directly related to everyday life.

As Poet Katrina McCain dives into fictional stories of heroic tales, she leaves you itching to flip each page. The connection you will feel to the characters and storyline is a bond created by the shared emotions between you and Poet Katrina McCain.

Enjoy your favorite drink out of your Poet Katrina McCain mug and enjoy the rollercoaster of suspense, mystery, and adventure!

Arrius L McCain
Greensboro, NC
9/27/2023

Acknowledgments

All praises belong to **God** for doing things beyond my imagination and expectations! I am forever grateful he chose me to be the recipient of the gift of words. Thank you, God, that I completed my third book when I never had plans to write one. Like always, situations happened while I was working on this project, but God provided a way for it to be completed beautifully and flawlessly. This journey has been absolutely amazing, and I thank God for being there every step of the way!

Arrius McCain... Thank you always for holding me down regardless of the situation we faced individually or as a family! I appreciate your entrepreneurial spirit and how it motivates me to stay on top of my game. Thanks for your opinion, approval, and ideas for this project! I love you from the bottom of my heart and thanks for being the best son I could have ever asked for!

Angela McCain... Thank you Pumpkin Boo for being my biggest cheerleader no matter what! The pride beaming from your eyes when you look at me makes me want to continue to do better and be better for you. Thank you for helping me come up with names for my characters and giving me extra time on Game Nights to finish writing. Hearing you say you want to be just like me is the biggest compliment, and I always tell you I want you to be better!

Lorraine Sessoms... Thank you Mommy for making me feel like you were always in my corner, and I could count on you! My family and I appreciate you always. Thanks again for checking in on the progress on this book. Your check-ins reminded me of deadlines I missed or ones coming up. You helped to keep me on track, and I am not sure you even know that. Thank you for holding me accountable!

Adolphus McCain... Your love was so sweet and genuine that it has lasted years beyond your death. I try to walk in a way that represents you well and make you proud to have been my dad. Your teachings shape my writing style as I try to be the lady you taught me to be even on paper. I miss you beyond words. Until we meet again...

Leroy Sessoms... Thank you for loving me the way you loved me! I was always able to count on you to help me even in the messes I created. Being a Stepdad was not a word you used as you introduced me, and I appreciate being treated as your daughter always. Thank you over and over again for the love and support!

To my Sisters... Thanks for being my rocks in good and bad times! No matter what we faced in life, we have always known we had someone in our corner wanting the best for us. I love you sisters for who you are in my life. Thank you for being my motivation and inspiration when you had no idea you were. My love runs deep for you and there is nobody like my amazing sisters!

Nieces and Nephews... You continue to make me proud of you by the way you live your lives and how you handle your responsibilities. You make life look easy as you conquer the world so flawlessly. Thanks for loving on your Auntie and making me feel special! I promise it means more to me than you would ever know.

My Girls... You feel more like sisters than friends and I appreciate your friendship, love, and support! When I am having a tough time, one of you reach out unexpectedly. You have been there for me through thick and thin, and I count it a blessing to have been friends with you as long as we have been. Keep on loving on me as I continue to love on you!

Carlos Kaigler aka The Poet B.GKL... Thank you for planting the seed for this project. Based off my previous writings, you told me several times you had faith I could write a short story book and you challenged me to do so with the title, **"Fragile Love with Glass Affections."** As a result, it turned out to be a masterpiece and the fire was lit to write my first short story book. Thanks for always being solid, reliable, and a great friend!

Introduction

Words float around the world waiting for us to grab hold of them to express matters of the heart. I bravely decided to place those words on paper, with excitement, for a third time with my first short story book. I would like to introduce to you *"One Day Things Changed: Fictional Short Stories about Love, Betrayal and Redemption"* as a feel-good book meant for entertainment and enlightenment.

"One Day Things Changed" was birthed from a friend's challenge for me to write a short story. He observed something special in my writing and encouraged me to expand my horizons beyond poetry. Since I enjoy most writing styles, I accepted the challenge to see what I could create. Surprisingly, I wrote a short story that turned out amazing and I began to think about writing my first short story book. With the completion of each story, my confidence rose, and I knew I could do this.

My imagination reached across several genres and *"One Day Things Changed"* can be summed up as a contemporary fiction. **"Loving Unconditionally"** chapters include a hopeless romance and a powerful family drama. You will fall in love with the characters and sympathize with their

1

situations. **"Webs Of Betrayal"** chapters contain a despicable heartbreak, a gut-wrenching true crime, and a captivating fantasy short story. You will be compelled to remember better days are ahead as you tap into your imagination to walk on the wild side. The **"Finding Redemption"** chapter contains an unpredictably short story that encourages you to believe in people, hope, and faith again.

In the chaotic world in which we live, I offer a relatable and enjoyable short story book that will cause you to laugh, cry, or pray for the characters. I wrote this book in a way in which everyone could see themselves in the stories and wish for the best outcome possible. Regardless of the year the story was set, each short story has a present-day theme and can easily fit into today's trials and struggles.

After reading this short story book, I want readers to feel the authenticity and genuineness in what I have written. I want them to recognize the originality in each story and enjoy my creative thoughts as I wrote outside the box. I want the readers to feel good about their book purchase from me and look forward to future projects. Finally, I would like the readers to feel motivated and encouraged to pursue their dreams by recognizing if I can do it, so can they.

Welcome to my newest creation offered in the form of a short story book! I pray you enjoy every short story as you take another wild roller coaster ride with me. If you enjoyed my previous poetry books, *"**Because She Decided to Love**"* and *"**Then The Unexpected Happened**"*, I am confident you will enjoy *"**One Day Things Changed**".* Buckle up, enjoy yourself, and happy reading!

Chapter I:

Loving Unconditionally

* * *

Abbie's Hidden Desire

Abbie rushed around the corner to see a line of people waiting to enter the 2019 National Comic Book Convention hosted by Graphics. People were dressed in all kinds of costumes while yelling obscenities at Abbie but none of them would answer her questions about the VIP entrance. Her email stated she should enter through the VIP entrance as part of her upgraded package. As she continued to bypass more patrons, the VIP Entrance signs became visible as sweat ran down her back. Abbie was extremely glad she did not wear her costume as she had in past years. The outfits were ruined before the Meet and Greet began.

The full VIP experience at this convention gave Abbie access to a private changing room with champagne, fruit, and chocolate. The extra money she paid was well worth it. Transforming into her favorite character, Kandy, once a year, was a worthy experience. Abbie and Kandy both have secret identities, and they both loved to save the underdog. Abbie had an unhealthy obsession with Graphics' comic book, so much so, that she was the originator behind Kandy's social media page followed by millions. At her CPA firm, Abbie gravitated towards the clients needing Forensic Accounting Assistance. She liked uncovering the person who committed fraud or embezzled money, and this type of accounting was her specialty.

In the comic book, Kandy worked as a nurse in a low budget hospital with inadequate supplies in an under-privileged neighborhood. According to her co-workers, she missed huge chunks of her workdays and was not responsible. Little did they know, she heard 911 distress calls over the police radio located in the ER Department, and she would leave work to help. The Graphics' writers put Kandy in the right spot at the right time to assist with capturing the bad guys. Her character was relatable and so lovable that she was liked by everyone who fell in love with the comic book.

Smiling at her reflection in the mirror, Abbie was satisfied she switched up her costume to resemble what Kandy wore in the 115th Special Edition released by Graphics. She wore the 5-inch red thigh-high boots in place of the 3-inch calf boots usually worn by Kandy. Instead of the red shimmery top Kandy typically wore, Abbie wore a red halter top with a black push up bra leaving nothing to the imagination. She finished the look with Kandy's usual mid-thigh black leather skirt with splits on both sides. With the mask securely in place and her glowing red lipstick, Abbie had more body parts exposed than she had hidden.

She winked at the sexiest version of Kandy she had ever dressed as and pranced out of her VIP room as her body parts jingled. Abbie gracefully walked through the conference room during the Meet and Greet looking for others dressed as her favorite characters. She introduced herself and shared small talk with them and suddenly the expensive four-hour plane ride with a crying baby was worth it. Unexpectedly, she was drawn to a man about six feet tall dressed as Titus, who is Kandy's love interest in the Graphics' comic book.

This man dressed as Titus was in the corner of the room with a drink in his hand as Abbie fought a hidden desire to play with him. She wanted to believe her attraction to him was based on Kandy and Titus' relationship; however, she was captivated by his aura. Boldly making her way to him, the most beautiful smile under his mask greeted her from across the room. Glued to the spot next to him, Abbie was unable to tear herself away from him for the rest of the evening. She was so fascinated by his opinion of Kandy and Titus' love story, and she loved his enthusiasm for both characters.

He was not ready to release Abbie from his presence as the final announcements for the evening replaced the music playing through the speakers. He extended an invitation to Abbie to meet him on the rooftop of their hotel in an hour. Hoping to spice things up, she accepted his invite with one condition. They do not exchange information of who they really were. Agreeing to the terms as she hoped he would, this gentleman remained Titus. Abbie loved how her plan to play with a hidden desire this weekend was unfolding.

Delighted she packed a second set of provocative clothes, Abbie had no idea she would wear them or pull them out of the suitcase. Excitedly, she laid the black leather body suit on the bed before she showered. The low cleavage one piece hugged all the right spots, showing off the progress made at the gym on nights she did not want to go. Abbie decided to wear the red thigh-high boots and finished the look with her red glowing lipstick that Titus complimented several times throughout the night.

Dressed as Kandy's devilish twin, Abbie's sureness led the way to the rooftop with a glass of champagne in her hand. She wanted his compliments to continue to fuel the hidden desire within her all night long. Abbie exited the elevator to see a familiar smile waiting for her arrival. Titus hugged her tightly as he whispered how amazing she looked and felt in his arms. Feeling the sexual tension growing to a level she had never experienced before, Abbie shocked herself by staying in a flirtatious zone.

Their conversation picked up where it left off at the Meet and Greet room as their hands and bodies explored each other more intimately. Titus carefully responded to Abbie hoping not to come on too strong. While walking towards her room, she knew then she was not ready for him to stop talking to her or him touching her. Abbie could hear

Titus' body telling her loud and clear that he was ready and willing to do whatever she was willing and ready to do. Each touch from his lips, the tip of his nose, the end of his beard, his hands, and the growing member from down below made it harder for Abbie to fight her hidden desire.

Not wanting to wait a couple of hours to see him again, she looked him directly in his eyes and told him to join her on the other side of the door. Giving into the heat between them, Abbie and Titus' love scene extended far beyond the Graphics writers' creativity. Titus did not stop holding her hands or kissing her gently on the cheek before going off into the sunset like he usually did. Nothing was PG-13 about the script written by two lovers in the early morning hours, as they declared themselves the greatest superheroes ever to exist.

Plastered against the wall with Titus' arms around her, Abbie had never felt sexier, and Titus discerned it was time to extinguish the fire he started. Abbie began to act out the motions she imagined Kandy would, if ever in this position with Titus. She climbed the wall and provided a new wave for him to ride with her. The coolness from the wall and the heat from Titus caused Abbie to succumb, as Kandy did when the enemy figured out her weakness. Slowly being lowered to the floor, Abbie concluded that Titus did not leave one area burning before they peeled off the wall.

Waking up in Titus' arms a few hours later, Abbie looked around the room trying to focus her eyes. She had a hangover from the wall climbing, intertwining with Titus, and drinking several glasses of wine. The clock beamed 7:29 am and the 2019 National Comic Book Convention hosted by Graphics restarted at 8:00 am. Day 2 consisted of breakfast between 8:00 am-9:00 am and a meeting with the writers of the comic book at 9:30 am to learn what was next for each character. Abbie was eager to attend all the events; however, playing with a hidden desire disabled her ability to think straight or worry about her lack of sleep.

As if reading her mind, Titus held her tightly and started nibbling on her ears and neck. He decided to feast on what was right in front of him and enjoyed their tardiness. Tearing themselves away from each other for Titus to go to his room to dress was difficult, but they agreed on meeting thirty minutes later downstairs to walk the couple blocks to the Convention Center. Shivering at how aggressive she was with Titus and how confidently he took charge, Abbie was ready for more quiet time with him.

Abbie closed her eyes as she was mesmerized by their collaboration in the shower when she should be concentrating on not being late for their meet-up. With each brushstroke of her makeup brush, she imagined Titus caressing her face as gently as she applied the golden blush on her cheeks and the amber eye color on her eye lids. His sensual scent overpowered the expensive bottle of perfume she sprayed on her neck, chest, and thighs as he left pieces of himself everywhere in her room.

Moments to spare before the writers' roundtable panel; Abbie made two cups of coffee and grabbed croissants and fruit left from breakfast, while Titus found a table with two available seats. They did not miss much other than mingling with the other Graphics' fans during breakfast. Fascinated with the depth each writer gave to the characters' development and the story lines during the discussion, Abbie anticipated one of them finally exploring the magical connection between Kandy and Titus.

The writers could leave the fans guessing, as they have for twenty years, or they could write love scenes like Kandy and Titus shared last night and this morning. Any scene the two characters starred in together, brought complete happiness to the fans long after they obtained the bad guys for the police to arrest. Love was sprinkled delicately in the thin pages of the comic book and the crackling of another fantasy between the two of them was written in history forever.

During the afternoon break, Titus and Abbie went sightseeing throughout the city. They honored the agreement not to exchange names and getting to know each other on a more personal level was effortless despite the rule. They talked about family, their careers, their biggest challenges in life, their goals, and their excitement of meeting each other. Their hidden desire for one another was brewing the entire afternoon as Abbie leaned in extremely close to Titus. She softly whispered to him that they should begin a different panel discussion where they were the guest panelists.

Before the words could leave her lips completely, Abbie was blowing warm air in Titus' ear, and he could feel the whirlwind beginning. Just like Kandy did numerous times, Abbie was setting the atmosphere the way she wanted it to be by controlling the wind. Over the last twelve hours or more, Abbie learned when to be forceful or temperamental for her superpower to work effectively on Titus. Having time to explore another cyclone with Titus before the next event, Abbie's exhaustion stayed at bay and did not ruin the moment.

She explored every fantasy she had for Titus, her long-time crush, from her reading Graphics' comic book from twelve years old to now. Looking for someone to spark the same kind of fires Titus did, she was left unsatisfied with the dating scene. She never had the self-assurance to embrace the full sexiness of Kandy until this conference. Fortunately for Abbie, tangible things in his hotel room were laced with the flames of Titus fires and circulated by Kandy's twisters. Abbie did not play fairly as she quenched her hidden desire on the bed, on the table, on the floor, and on the bathroom sink.

Abbie left Titus to prepare for the formal dinner scheduled for 8:00 pm. This was her favorite part of the convention as everyone was required to dress in formal wear with no masks. She lived a dull life outside of the Graphics' conventions and Abbie rarely had a reason to dress in a beautiful gown like the one she purchased for this event. She enjoyed her nice long bubble bath before getting dressed for the evening. Abbie missed Titus' presence, warm embrace, flattery words, and his smooth voice.

Craving his touch and wanting his endless approval, Abbie hurried to get dressed and headed to the formal dance. Her custom black, silk evening gown flowed elegantly down the couple of blocks to the Graphics' Convention Center. The wind showed Abbie off in a way that twirling around on one leg could not do. She was stunning! Her fit and flare design went perfectly with the tiny straps framing her shoulders and hips impeccably. Her hanging necklace showed off the length of her neck. Her tear-drop earrings added a glamorous touch taking her entire ensemble to another level.

Looking at her silhouette on the glass building as she walked to the entrance, she was sexy in the full-length gown as she embodied Kandy's persona. She was bold, confident, in charge, held her head a little higher as she walked, and simply gorgeous. Abbie slid on her evening gloves moments before entering the building and she noticed she was a little nervous. She greeted the people she met in past years, which calmed her raging nerves, as Titus worked the other side of the room without taking his eyes off her.

With at least forty people standing between them, their smiles found each other across the room several times. Abbie read the words coming from Titus' lips saying she was exquisite. She smiled as she continued to talk, dance, and enjoy the other people at the convention. Running into a friend she met previously, she was shocked they had not seen each other before that night. Knowing her own masterplan of playing with a hidden desire with Titus in all her free time was the sole reason, Abbie changed the subject from her absence to a memory of them both arriving in similar Kandy outfits before.

Not able to wait, Titus found Abbie and greeted her by holding her hands and kissing her gently on the cheek for the first time that evening. Abbie's friend wanted to know who the handsome gentlemen was, and all the details of their relationship. The formal dinner was beginning, which included honoring the creators of Graphics and the accolades were well deserving. Celebrating the milestones set by Graphics, Abbie was applauding the momentous time she was having overall. The events were well organized, the food was amazing, the music was enjoyable, and Abbie played with a hidden desire more times than she could count with Titus.

Vendors lined the walls outside of the conference room selling merchandise related to Graphics' comic book. Abbie wandered from vendor to vendor looking for unique artifacts or souvenirs to take home with her. She understood her greatest souvenir would be the amazing memories of Titus and her as they intertwined with wind and fire in their superhero world. Abbie then purchased a shirt from one of the vendors and bumped into someone after placing her arm through the bag she was given. She was ecstatic when she recognized it was Titus and her sultry game of seduction beckoned him to her.

Her worthy partner stood directly before her, and she could already feel the heat from his fire. Immediately, he grabbed her hands and kissed her softly on the cheek. Abbie's heart flipped and flopped at his touch, and she could not react the way she was feeling as people were around them. Together, Abbie and Titus visited more vendors as their conversation picked up from earlier in the evening. In the far corner, a photographer had a Graphics' logo as the backdrop, and Titus then begged Abbie to take pictures with him.

Posing next to each other was so naturally smooth. The photographer had rarely seen such chemistry like this in his career. Abbie acted like a professional model as her body responded to Titus' body, by changing poses for the camera. Steam could be felt by everyone witnessing the magic happening and whispers began among the crowd as who the power couple was. As the crowd grew bigger and the photographer's smiled grew wider, Abbie and Titus ended their photography session with their classic greeting of Titus holding her hands and kissing her gently own the cheek.

The photographer gathered their information to deliver the pictures in a couple of days and he asked Abbie and Titus how long have they been dating or how long have they been married. He explained the natural way they took pictures without instructions was as top tier as it came in the business, and it took a couple of years to master that level of technique together. Abbie was stunned by the photographer's admiration and question. She told him they have been flirting with one another for twenty years and she was waiting to see how their story would unfold with a wink.

The photographer turned the camera in Abbie and Titus' directions. He was ready to share their pictures with them immediately. Wind and fire have never been captured so beautifully as Abbie and Titus agreed with the photographer about the greatness captured on film. Standing next to Titus, listening to the compliments from the crowd, she could feel another fire brewing within her and all she wanted was to play with a hidden desire with Titus as the leading male.

Abbie was excited from knowing the night would end amazingly as they walked to the elevator together. Entering Titus' room, Abbie felt as comfortable around his things as she felt around hers. She poured them both a glass of wine and Titus stared deeply at her as he grabbed his glass. Not having a chance to dance with Abbie at the formal dinner, he asked her to dance with him before placing their glasses on the table. Abbie closed the gap between the two of them as Titus put his arms on the lower part of her back. Swaying to the invisible beat created by the intense fire between them, Abbie turned her back to Titus after what felt like a lifetime of waiting for a moment like this.

Firmly pressed against his chest, she closed her eyes so she could feel him with all her senses. Interlocking her fingers with his, Abbie stepped away far enough for him to see the seductive dance moves she was doing. Seconds later, Abbie felt Titus lift her into the air heading towards the bathroom. Slowly, using her nails to scratch down Titus' chest as she mounted him was driving him crazy. Her alter-ego surprised her as she found herself doing and saying things, she never envisioned herself saying to anyone.

Abbie enjoyed the pure satisfaction on his face as she controlled the tempo in the shower. For the first time in Graphics' history, Titus was completely controlled by someone else's superpower. Carefully taken care of him during his weaken state, she slowly increased the tempo as she and Titus flew above the skies in their super world. The moonlit journey, with Abbie being the best tour guide, lasted until she could not play with the winds created by her hidden desire.

Abbie's dreadful alarm roared through the room, and she did not want to move from being tucked under Titus' body. Her exhaustion from the entire weekend had finally set in, as she remembered the wrap up brunch for the final day of the convention. She needed to head to her own room to pack her things, shower, get dressed for the day, and head to the convention center. Slowing moving from each other, Abbie braced herself as Titus held her hands and kissed her gently on the cheek. Looking into his eyes at the entryway of his hotel door, Abbie was very fond of the person she spent the most time with in a very long time.

Abbie did not regret anything that happened between Titus and her the weekend thus far and was looking forward to the last couple of hours she would have with him. Entering the Breakfast Hall of the convention center, she spotted the seats Titus had secured near the stage for the final panel discussion taking place during brunch. She signaled to him that she had seen him, and Abbie made her way to him. Holding her hands and kissing her gently on the cheek, Abbie told him good morning again with a hug. She handed her luggage to him so he could get it checked into the holding area until they were ready to leave.

Abbie spoke to everyone at the table as she sipped on the coffee directly in front of her. Titus rejoined them at the table as brunch was served at other tables. The panel discussion was motivational as more Graphics' writers shared their humble beginnings. Abbie never felt prouder to be a part of this super hero world more than she did right now. New ideas ran through her mind wanting to revamp Kandy's social media page as soon as she secretly could. Abbie concluded the 2019 National Comic Book Convention was the best one she attended thus far, and it was partially due to the intense love affair between Kandy and Titus.

Standing in line together at the airport, Abbie and Titus continued to enjoy one another as they waited to get through security. Their chemistry had others around them smiling as they were electric standing near one another. Titus continued to have his hands on Abbie in some capacity, either holding her lower back or her hand. Walking to her gate and placing her luggage beside her, Abbie leaned in for Titus to hold her hands and kiss her gently on the cheek. She melted in his embrace as she enjoyed the person she became when she was with him.

Her actions were completely out of the normal for her and she was glad he agreed to them not knowing each other's real names the entire weekend. Starting a romantic relationship the way she was with Titus was something the older ladies in her family preached against her entire life. Her actions did not seem to faze Titus as he adoringly called her his Sweet Kandy one last time. Becoming her alter-ego was exhausting and Abbie was pleased how well she played the role. Finally resting in her seat as she waited for the plane to take off, Abbie blew out a deep breath hoping to recover from the weekend.

Finding the perfect playlist on her phone, she closed her eyes to dreams of Titus and more adventures they could have. Turbulence jolted her out of her sleep, and she had no idea how much time was left on the flight. She kept her eyes opened long enough to put her phone in her pocket so she would not drop it, but something was blocking a smooth entry. Abbie had no idea what it could be; she only worn the jacket a couple of times. Pulling out the crumbled business card; Abbie smiled as she read Titus' name was James, he was an engineer, and he lived in the next state from hers. Placing the card on her chest, Abbie was thankful James did not listen to her as she drifted off to sleep again.

Two years later, Abbie and James welcomed their family and friends to their wedding rehearsal dinner. They were planning to get married tomorrow evening and start the second half of their lives together. The 2019 National Comic Book Convention brought more than fans together with their favorite writers, it brought two people together who loved one another on paper for far too long without putting action behind the attraction. Tomorrow evening, Abbie and James planned to rewrite the history of the classic love story between Kandy and Titus as they say I do.

* * *

Grandma Pearl

and

The Summer of 1949

"My granddaughter and Cindy have got something coming to them," stated Grandma Pearl, "if they are going to gyrate to music all night and catch up on beauty sleep all day." They were sneaking down to The Hill where all the new music was being played, just like her best friend and she did when she was their age. Grandma Pearl understood how hard it was to park your hips in one of them seats as the music does not stop until your feet were moving on the dance floor. The dishes were washed and put away, and a note was on the refrigerator that read, "tomorrow night's dinner in the fridge." So, that was all the ruckus she heard from the kitchen last night.

Grandma Pearl wondered out loud with no one listening in particular, "hmmm... we will see how long this good behavior stuff lasts for these two." Standing in the kitchen leaning against the countertop, Grandma Pearl was equally impressed as she was upset. She had not seen Mattie or Cindy yet, and it was time to get started on the chores. No young lady should be in bed past this time of the morning as the menfolk had gone to the field hours ago. "Those girls have to get up, and I mean right now," Grandma Pearl uttered.

She walked down the hallway to find something to put in her hands as she wanted Mattie and Cindy to see how serious she was when she entered their bedroom. "Ah huh," voiced Grandma Pearl as she grabbed her husband's cane sitting next to the coat rack. Grandma Pearl's masterplan was to whack some sense into Mattie and Cindy with the cane if they did not move when she called their names. Grandma Pearl knocked on the door and screamed, "Get up girls. Your Grandpa Robert will be back for lunch in a few, and I cannot have y'all still asleep."

There was no movement from Mattie's side of the bed, but Cindy sprung up like a chicken. Grandma Pearl laughed and assumed that Cindy must have heard the conversation she had in the kitchen so Cindy sprung up so she would not receive this nice old butt whipping this morning. "Mattie! Cindy! You have about thirty minutes to get up from them beds! Go brush your teeth! And meet me in the kitchen!" Looking around the room that was not filthy, Grandma Pearl was impressed again by the girls and could not fuss at them too much.

Grandma Pearl was not sure what they were going to do first, seeing that the girls had supper prepared already. Next, they prepared lunch for Grandpa Robert and the field hands and started on the preserves for the winter. It was always plenty to do when those men were in the field, and Mattie wondered how her Grandma Pearl got it all done when she was not visiting. After preparing the preserves, Grandma Pearl asked Mattie and Cindy to have a seat at the table with her. They were going to take a break over tea and cookies.

These moments are what Mattie loved the most about staying with her Grandparents over the summers and during her school breaks. They always took the time to bestow wisdom on her, and the life lessons they gave her were treasured. Grandma Pearl wanted to talk about reputation and how it could affect someone years later. She was worried how the two young girls going to The Hill to listen to music and gyrating all times of the night looked to other people. After Mattie and Cindy received the advice on how to be ladies, Mattie extended an offer to Grandma Pearl.

Mattie asked her to join them to see what the hype was all about at The Hill. Cindy explained to Grandma Pearl different local singers, poets, and dancers perform every night and The Hill's stage is where some of them catch their big break. After much persuasion, Grandma Pearl hesitantly agreed to go with them. Dinner had to be served and the kitchen had to be cleaned first. She was no stranger to having fun; however, Grandma Pearl always worried about her granddaughter having the right kind of fun so her reputation and future would not suffer.

Grandma Pearl looked through her closet for the perfect outfit to wear. She rarely went out on the town, and she had no idea how the young people dressed these days. After freshening up, Grandma Pearl decided on a dress and some heels that she wore years ago when she and Grandpa Robert danced the night away. Ready earlier than agreed upon with the girls, Grandma Pearl decided to go on the front porch and enjoy the fresh night air until they were ready. The night was beautiful and full of opportunities.

Grandpa Robert joined Grandpa Pearl as he handed her a cup of tea. Waking up to her for fifty-eight years, she remained the woman of his dreams and she was as beautiful as the day he met her. Grandpa Robert told her he did not know how he was so lucky that God gave her to him to love and cherish for the rest of his life. As Grandma Pearl blushed at his tender words, the girls came onto the front porch to witness love at its best. Grandpa Robert put everyone in a great mood as they kissed and hugged him goodbye before they got in the car.

It was Poetry Night at The Hill, and the stage was dedicated to all poets in the building to express themselves however they chose to do so. Mattie and Cindy signed up to sing together since the MC inserted other entertainers in open slots throughout the night. Mattie, Cindy, and Grandma Pearl were enjoying a dance on the dance floor when they called Ms. Pearl to the stage to perform next. Mattie and Cindy turned to each other and questioned whether Ms. Pearl was the same Ms. Pearl as in their Grandma Pearl.

Their question was answered as Grandma Pearl made her way to the stage. Completely speechless and cheering in awe; Mattie watched her Grandma Pearl walk onto the stage, and she hung onto every word she spoke thereafter. Grandma

Pearl was elegant and nice with her poetic flow, and gentle and precise with the delivery of each word. With her eyes closed during the entire performance, Mattie knew Grandma Pearl missed how the crowd was so in tune with her, and they fell in love with her poetry with one poem just like she did.

Mattie and Cindy ran to the side of the stage when Grandma Pearl was done performing. "Grandma Pearl, you were great!" exclaimed Mattie. "Grandma Pearl, I did not know you had that in you," said Cindy. Grandma Pearl whispered to them both, "that is how I got Grandpa Robert's attention with his fine self and all of those fast-tailed women in town wanting him." Giggling together as they made their way back to their tables, Mattie heard Cindy and her name being called to come to the stage.

Grandma Pearl wanted to see what this was about. She only heard her granddaughter humming around the house before. Grandma Pearl would hear her sing for the first time; Mattie was nervous, and Cindy sensed it too. Cindy winked at Mattie with assurance and mouthed the words, "you got this!" Mattie came in on cue with the bridge following Cindy's opening verse. The girls sang the chorus together as tears flowed down Grandma Pearl's face. When Mattie sang the second verse, Grandma Pearl was standing on her feet and clapping as loudly as she could.

Once they finished singing, Grandma Pearl rushed to meet the girls in the same spot they met her when she finished her poetry. She hugged and kissed each of them as her pride for them beamed throughout the building. "When did y'all learn to sing like that?" questioned Grandma Pearl. Mattie and Cindy told her they loved to sing, which is the reason they elected to take Chorus in school. They became best friends in the class and supported each other with their singing engagements outside of it. Their love for certain songs and artists is why they started singing together and now they rarely perform without each other.

Mattie and Cindy were known as "Love's Connection" on campus and around their town and were respected as two of the hottest singers around. Both girls told Grandma Pearl their parents supported their singing group and them touring locally. "Grandma Pearl, I have been scared to tell Grandpa Robert and you. I did not know how you would feel about me performing," explained Mattie. Grandma Pearl squeezed her hand and said, "Baby, you can tell your grandma anything. What I just heard shows how fine of women you and Cindy are."

Mattie had no idea her Grandma Pearl was a poet, and her secret of being a singer was out of the bag as well. Her heart was full on the drive home as everyone enjoyed the quietness of the night. Cindy helped Grandma Pearl out of the car and onto the front porch as Mattie put the car in the garage. Grandpa Robert met them at the door waiting to hear the details about their night. Grandma Pearl bragged about Mattie and Cindy like the proudest grandmother in the world. She further explained how she misjudged the girls about their gyrating all night long, and she now looked at it as the girls pursuing their dreams.

Mattie thanked Grandma Pearl with tears in her eyes. Mattie told Grandpa Robert how majestically Grandma Pearl recited her poem and how she seemed to have no fear when she stepped on the stage. Cindy told Grandpa Robert the crowd loved her immediately, and how she received a standing ovation. He told Mattie and Cindy she had the same effect on him and that is why he had to marry her. Grandpa Robert was proud of his girls, and he was so glad Grandma Pearl experienced their world for one night.

The sun shined a little brighter throughout the house as everyone was still on a high. Grandma Pearl woke the girls up in her usual way, and they both smiled when she walked out of the room. "What a difference a night could make?" Mattie said to Cindy as they dressed for the day. Last night broke misunderstood ideas from both generations, and Grandma Pearl and Mattie were glad for the breakthrough. Joining Grandma Pearl at the kitchen table for coffee, Mattie witnessed she was moving a little slower and worried she kept her out too late.

Mattie asked Grandma Pearl how she was feeling and if everything was ok. Grandma Pearl answered with the same response she always answered with, "I'm fine baby! Do not be worrying yourself about me." Grandma Pearl helped Mattie and Cindy finished the usual chores around the house, despite their constant pleading for her to let them finish everything. Finally giving in to the tiredness, Grandma Pearl made her secret cure-all tea and took a break after all.

As soon as the evening news went off, everyone met at the kitchen table for Game Night. Grandpa Robert noticed the dimness in Grandma Pearl's eyes and asked her if she was feeling well. She shook her head yes, and Cindy told him they had been worried about her all day given that she was moving slower than usual. Mattie told him she should not have insisted that Grandma Pearl join Cindy and her last night. Grandpa Robert told them both how much it meant to

Grandma Pearl, and she had not talked about anything as long and with so much excitement.

Grandpa Robert told the girls not to regret anything, as he felt like last night was needed and was necessary. Grandpa Robert released Mattie and Cindy's hands and told them to stop holding up the butt whippings they were going to receive during Game Night. Laughter could be heard miles down the road, and love could be felt towns over.

Mattie woke up before she heard her Grandma Pearl outside her bedroom trying to find something to put in her hand to wake Cindy and her up. Completely ready for the day, she was surprised she had not seen Grandma Pearl yet. Mattie pondered, "look at what time it is. She should have been here ten times by now rushing us along." Mattie told Cindy she was going to get the day started in the kitchen the minute she checked on Grandma Pearl. Cindy expressed to Mattie, "maybe she slept in. She was tired yesterday." Mattie shrubbed her shoulders, hoping she was overthinking things, and decided to head out of the bedroom in search of Grandma Pearl.

It did not seem like her not to be moving about already. Maybe she started her day outside in the garden before her tasks in the kitchen. Searching the kitchen, pantry, garden, and the rest of the yard, Mattie and Cindy were not able to find Grandma Pearl anywhere. Growing concern was causing Mattie to worry about Grandma Pearl's condition. Mattie looked at Cindy and said, "Grandma Pearl's bedroom."

Both girls headed towards the house in a full sprint. Playfully, Mattie began whispering to Grandma Pearl the best lines she heard this summer as Grandma Pearl laid in the bed. "Do you know you are late, young lady, and that is not right. You cannot be gyrating those hips all night and cannot get up the next day. Get up now! I have this cane in my hand, and I'm not scared to use it, young lady!" repeated Mattie. Now that the room was brighter from Cindy pulling back the curtains, Mattie perceived something was not right. Shaking Grandma Pearl backward and forward by the shoulders, Mattie screamed, "GRANDMA PEARL, GET UP!"

Grandpa Robert walked in the bedroom door as Mattie was screaming and put his arms around her. She explained to him through sobs, "Grandpa Robert, something has happened to Grandma Pearl. She is not moving or anything when I call her name. I cannot feel her breath or feel her heart beating when I put my head on her chest." Getting through the explanation was tougher than anything she had ever done before. Grandpa Robert told Mattie to let him check Grandma Pearl out as he slowly released her from his embraced.

Immediately, Mattie reached for Cindy and the two of them hugged each other until there was news about Grandma Pearl. Checking for a heartbeat and a pulse, Grandpa Robert told the girls Grandma Pearl had never responded this way to a bug before. He performed a brief examination and told the girls as gently as he could that Grandma Pearl had passed on. He held both girls to prevent them from falling to the floor from the shock of the news.

Hours later, there was much commotion from the EMTs, the Coroner's Office, and the Police Department coming into the house to figure out what happened to Grandma Pearl. Immediate family members, including Mattie's parents, and the field hands started to show up at the house for support. Cindy was super polite and helpful by asking everyone if they wanted water or coffee. She also prepared lunch for everyone and constantly restocked the refreshments.

Everyone asked Grandpa Robert and Mattie the same questions in different ways and their answers did not change. "Did she have any aliments or take medications? When did Grandma Pearl start feeling bad? What were her symptoms?

When did she eat last and what was it? What time did she go to bed, and was that early for her? Did she move about during the night? What time did she normally get up in the mornings? Did she sleep in late from time to time? Was she in any pain or complained about any discomfort? How active has she been lately? Did you talk to her before going to the field?" questioned the officials.

Mattie and Grandpa Robert's answers seemed rehearsed, but the truth was the truth. "No aliments, she takes a multivitamin every day, yesterday morning, tiredness, she did not eat dinner, breakfast nor lunch well, so maybe two days ago, she had pot roast, she went to bed around 7:00 pm, that is early for her when Mattie is visiting, she did not move too much throughout the night other than a bathroom break, she is normally awake and dressed no later than 6:00 am, she never slept in, she did not complain about pain or discomfort even with slower reactions from her, she is usually very active for her age with an exception to yesterday, and I kissed her as I said goodbye, and she smiled at me," explained Mattie and Grandpa Robert.

Mattie's parents were able to piece together the story from the last couple of days of Grandma Pearl's life from listening to Grandpa Robert and Mattie. Cindy filled in some details when emotions got the better of them. There were times when the authorities had to wait a few minutes to hear what happened next to Grandma Pearl. Cindy was caught up in emotions too. Immediately, the impact of her Grandma Pearl's death was heavily felt.

The house slowly began to clear out as the hours passed by. The immediate family migrated to the living room and started sharing their fondest memories of Grandma Pearl. Mattie was unable to speak when it felt like it was her turn to share with the family. She had not come to grips with the fact that Grandma Pearl would not be a part of her life anymore, and she could not articulate anything yet. All the changes she made within this summer with her grandparents have been remarkable.

Mattie grew more mature from the advice she received from her grandparents. She learned how to be more independent by storing up for the future due to its unpredictability. Mattie learned no matter how well you know someone, there are hidden things about them, until they are ready to reveal them. She learned to value her relationships more deeply as she had no idea when the other person would not be with her. Mattie learned there is nothing, she meant absolutely nothing, that could outweigh the love grandparents have for their grandchildren.

Mattie was finally ready to say to the rest of her family that the night Grandma Pearl, Cindy, and she shared at The Hill would forever be in her heart as one of the best nights of her life. Nothing could compare to the admiration she felt for her grandmother and the life lessons she bestowed on her. Mattie told her family with tears of joy that Grandma Pearl and the Summer of 1949 would forever be her fondest memories. She was grateful for the time she spent and the love she felt from her grandmother.

Chapter II:

Webs of Betrayal

* * *

Fragile Love with Glass Affections

I woke up with hazy glazed eyes and wondered exactly where I was before the ache in my heart reminded me of the recent events I wanted to forget. The weight of lies and deception rested heavily in the middle of my chest, and I did not want to move or breathe or think or feel. There was no way I had been receiving Fragile Love with Glass Affections for a year now. How can something so beautiful and strong have me torn up inside? A tear followed by more tears escaped my eyes as I squeezed them together tighter in hopes of stopping the steady stream now soaking my pillow.

After another soul cleansing cry, I glanced at my phone. I had seventy-two missed calls and two hundred and nine unanswered texts from the last five days that I have been running from the world. A couple of them were from my momma. She can sense when something is wrong with her baby. Have I been drowning in my sorrows behind a Fragile Love with Glass Affections?

I was too weak mentally to respond to any of the notifications on my phone. I tossed it on the other side of the bed with no interest as to where it landed. Feeling stupid and used by love, I gave into the raw emotions building inside of me. The last time I had an interest in doing anything was five nights ago when I pleaded for a position in her heart and in her life. When did the tables turn where I was cut from the shards of Glass Affections with Fragile Love?

Replaying the events in my mind of what landed me in this bed, I vividly recalled the night I met her. It was a cold January night, and the wind was blowing so strongly it cut through the night sky. I worked sixty-five hours the last two weeks straight and I was exhausted from everything involving those weeks. Each night of sleep felt like the night before where I slept for five minutes. My mind was in overdrive, along with having two influential clients with projects with the same deadline.

The take-out from multiple restaurants all tasted the same. The coffee tasted bland each morning and my work-out routine was neglected so I did not have the necessary energy to pass my front door. I did not know if I wore black suits each day to work or if I chose a variety of other colors. My suitcase was an extension of my body as it was within two feet of me. Before she and her Fragile Love with Glass Affections came into my life on a Friday night, I dozed off in the shower.

I was exhausted from looking at blueprints and all its revisions. I dreamed the clients rejected the perfect proposals and I had to repeat the last 3 months of work. I glanced at the clock several times once the sun started to rise the next morning. I needed to catch up on the gym sessions I skipped because of the demands at work the last two weeks. My bed held me hostage and I succumbed to its demands without a fight. When I finally decided I had enough sleep, the growl from my stomach echoed loudly throughout my condo.

How long have I been asleep? The ringing of my phone brought me out of my sleepy trance, and I immediately recognized the number. Catching up with one of my homeboys from college was always a great time. Several of us were free and we decided to go to the newly opened Grown and Sexy Lounge in town. All the reviews about the place were raving and there were lines around the block with people waiting to enter. The night was no exception as we waited thirty minutes to enter the lounge.

Immediately, I was impressed by the lounge's atmosphere and all the beautiful people it attracted. The lights were low, the music was dope, and the dance floor was crowded. Wanting to get my round of drinks out the way, I headed to the bar and placed the usual order for the crew. I laughed to myself because we have been friends for twenty years and nobody's drink orders have changed.

As I waited for the Bartender to return with our drinks, I saw the most beautiful creature I have ever seen, and I could not take my eyes off her. She was on the dance floor with two ladies, who looked to be her sisters, and a group of other beautiful ladies dancing to one of the latest Line Dancing Song. The way she swayed her hips and perked her lips to her moves caught my attention.

As soon as I put our drinks down on our table, I had to meet her. I sipped on my crisp cold beer, and I watched how the captivating lady commanded the room with her mannerisms. She was absolutely beautiful in the way she carried herself. She had on a tight black dress showing the right amount of thighs, which got me excited. The jacket she wore over the dress told me she was a classy lady, and a night club would not change how she presented herself to the world. Those three-inch heels she wore sealed the deal for me. She looked to be five foot and five inches tall with the prettiest light brown skin.

The club was dark and smoky from the effects the DJ used to make the atmosphere seem a little more appealing. The facade did not dull the radiance coming from her smile. Because I am just as extraordinary as she is, I made my move before she left with her girls. I quickly walked to her side of the club with no pickup line or pre-played conversation in mind. She did not deserve any line I used on another lady or any pickup line period.

I now stood only a foot away from her. I smiled at her as she turned in my direction and she smiled back. I extended my hand, introduced myself, and said, "It is nice to meet you." She grabbed my hand and seductively told me her name. I found myself smiling like a chess cat as I talked to her for the rest of the night. I intended to have her closer to me by leading her to the dance floor after getting her attention. The vibe between us was so strong, we exchanged numbers to keep in touch. Somehow, I missed the yellow neon sign flashing, "Warning: She is capable of Fragile Love with Glass Affections."

Months turned into a year as I began to know her deeper than any other love interest in my life. When things are going great for me in my personal life, my past or current lies always have a way of catching up to me. All my troubles began one night on a date with her. Interrupting the smooth R&B music playing throughout the sound system in my car, the dashboard screen displayed a familiar phone number. I ended the call with a button on the steering wheel, and now I probably had to face the skeletons in my closet.

Trying to remain cool, I did not acknowledge the phone call in hopes she would not say anything. Wrong! Her questions were so direct, I could not think of a lie to cover up or explain my after-hours phone call. I hesitantly answered her questions with spacing in between my words to avoid trapping myself. She told me to stop talking before she lost respect for me, and I knew our relationship had changed.

The car ride home was miserable and for the first time I could not read the vibes from my lady. The radio echoed louder inside the car and the streetlights flashed brighter outside the car. The secret of my other lover was supposed to go to the grave with me. I had no idea she would be this upset as she never pressed me about who I was with or where I was going. Splitting my time between two beautiful ladies did not mean I gave Fragile Love with Glass Affections to either of them. I gave both ladies the best of me, within reasonable limits, when I was with them. Now I stand at the crossroad I created, powerless and with no control.

Before the car came to a complete stop, she jumped out and slammed the door. I did not like seeing anyone hurting, especially me, behind my actions. I raced to her side of the car hoping to grab her before she reached her doorsteps. I have been in the position countless times when a lady screamed the very same words to me, "I do not want to ever see you again," but those words never stung like this before. Tears choked her words as she snatched from my embrace. I followed her up the steps before I decided to let things settle down for the night. Meanwhile, she slammed the door in my face.

Approaching thirty-five years old, it was probably time for me to settle down with one lady. I made progress when I settled down with just two ladies. Now with the truth of who I was and what I have been up to standing between us like an uninvited guest, I was paralyzed as to what to say. Days seemed like eternities before she took my phone call. She calmly said we needed to talk and asked if I could come over. I suggested we go to her favorite restaurant to have dinner and some wine to lessen the tension the conversation was surely going to bring. She disagreed and told me privacy would be best.

I played every possible scenario in my mind as to how the night would end. Would I end up with just one of my ladies in my life or would I end up in bed wrapped around her with all forgotten and forgiven? Only time would tell as I hoped cupid was on my side. I was willing to be completely honest during our conversations about my past life and the playthings I had in it. She might not have demanded anything of me if the dashboard in my car had not betrayed me.

Before I walked out the door to her house, I planned the perfect route to pick up her favorite wine, her favorite chocolate, a little "I'm sorry" gift, and arrive on time. I was nervous and felt like I was walking into a lion's den instead of one of my ladies' houses. I took deep breaths to calm my nerves and I reminded myself she loved me and was crazy about me as I was about her. I listened to my go-to-playlist in the car, and I felt better about the conversation I was going to have. I was not ready to leave my other lady, but I was willing to do whatever it took to keep her in my life.

She was extremely nervous, just like I was, when I walked through the front door. She had soft music playing and I could smell her favorite candle lingering in the air. She prepared dinner even though I offered a hundred times to stop for takeout. She was so amazing and was still willing to prepare dinner for me regardless of our breakup. We talked, made promises, set new ground rules, enjoyed a warm bath, I rubbed her feet, and we brought in the new day celebrating our relationship.

Our breakup would soon be a thing of our past and so was my other relationship if I wanted to keep "our new rules." The reconnection felt so great and new beginnings were ahead of us. There was no need to worry about all the minor details if we were on a good path to recovery. Should I have seen the writing on the wall to prevent me from laying in the bed in a cabin tucked away in the woods reminiscing over Fragile Love with Glass Affections?

As she slept so peacefully, my mind ran to the other side of town where my other lady was. I could not deny the physical connection I had with her, and it was like no physical connection I ever had with anyone. Our souls were attracted to each other with a magnetic force neither of us could explain. I never figured out if what we had was real or if our physical connection was Fragile Love with Glass Affections. We enjoyed the ride of our mutual understanding of not defining us with titles or labels and not asking questions when were not together. The relationship worked perfectly for the busy lifestyle I lived.

The next morning, we skipped our usual Saturday morning walk/run in the park we often did when we both had time. My heart and mind felt relieved, but I could not let go of the different vibe from her. She seemed closed off and guarded yet she smiled the same. Her eyes were not as warming and caring as they usually were. I chalked it up to the hurt caused by my actions and our new arrangement would take time. Every time I caught a glimpse of her eyes, the sickening feeling grew deeper in the pit of my stomach. I asked her if we were good throughout the morning, and she assured me we were fine.

Time went by and all seemed forgiven by her. We fell into a new groove which was better than before. I was proud to say I was truly a one lady's man, and I did not offer Fragile Love with Glass Affections. Dancing the night away with my lady, I told her I loved her, and I wanted a promising future between us. What I did not tell her was I planned the perfect proposal for her upcoming birthday. As we would overlook the balcony somewhere exotic, I would get on my knee and ask her to marry me.

I could not decide between three of the rings I picked so I reached out to her best friend for help. Getting her dad's permission for his daughter's hand in marriage was the last thing to make the perfect birthday for her and me. Things were amazing at work and at home and I could not be happier. I have never experienced that type of stability in my personal life, and I must admit, it felt good. Who was that new version of me, and could I trust the version of me even if I did not recognize it without the Fragile Love with Glass Affections holding my hand?

A couple of days before her birthday, I opened the front door of her place. Laughter and music greeted me as I turned the knob. I could have gone to my place and showered before coming over if she was entertaining. I peeked my head in the dining room and spoke to my lady and her friends. Putting my gym bag and jacket away, I decided to get a beer and find something on TV before I showered. Walking down the hallway, all the laughter stopped and the mood in the house shifted. Obviously, they were whispering about the latest gossip one of them heard.

As I turned to head back to her room so as not to invade their privacy, her best friend's voice rose a little higher and more aggressively than she meant for it. I heard her tell my lady, "Imagine how I felt helping him pick out a ring for you when I know your secret." My legs wanted to continue moving in the opposite direction or maybe out the front door, but I was glued to the floor. All I knew is I should not walk in the dining room to interrupt their conversation to keep my perfect relationship intact.

It was hard to un-hear the whispers carrying secrets she was hiding from me. She walked in her bedroom to ask if she could bring me anything and to tell me her girls would be leaving soon. I told her do not send her girls away and I was going home for the evening. Instantly knowing I heard their conversation, she excused herself to dismiss her friends. I heard whispers amongst them again and the house went quiet. What had she been up to, and would I be able to forgive her? My heart shattered at a Fragile Love with Glass Affections moment not initiated by me.

The only problem was I was the one getting cut. She started the conversation by saying she was not looking for what we developed when we met. I aggressively told her to get to the point and I was getting agitated by her stalling. Tears welled up in her eyes as she carefully explained her story of deception. Fragile Love with Glass Affections was not supposed to happen to me. Being a man with the best features and the perfect height, I never had problems attracting ladies or indecent propositions. Depending on the way the wind blew; I indulged in some, if not all, as the demands circled in the air.

I was carefree and I only participated in situations offering Fragile Love with Glass Affections. I was crushing the Architectural Business World and pursuing my own successful part-time Art Design Company. I had an eye for illustrating exactly what customers wanted and I went the extra mile to give it to them. Far from being an average man, I had many accolades hanging on my walls in the office and at home to prove how accomplished I was. I acknowledged my talent when rendering services to my customers but remained humbled by not bragging to my family and friends. Can Fragile Love with Glass Affections happen to a man like me?

I pulled in front of the logged cabin tucked away deep in the woods where only eight people knew it existed as my car dashboard said 12:15 am. My homeboys and I bought the getaway spot for moments like what I was going through, I guessed. I rushed through the door to find the bar fully stocked. I opened the first bottle of hard liquor I could find and straight to my mouth the bottle went. I hoped the smooth brown liquor could dull the pain taking over my soul. The conversation with her had me shaken as I found myself begging on my knees for hours for her not to leave me. I was sure we could make the situation work for all parties involved except her HUSBAND.

How could every touch, kiss, dance, dinner, or walk in the park be Fragile Love with Glass Affections? She explained her husband was overseas working and the relationship between us meant everything to her. She was lonely and I came into her life at the right time. She wanted to tell me the night the infamous call showed up on my car's dashboard, but she did not want a tick for tack situation. Her "Girls Trips" were to connect with her husband when she traveled domestically and internationally. How could I have not seen I was being lied to? Fragile Love with Glass Affections is what I do and not what gets done to me. I refused to believe our love was not strong enough to survive.

I fought for our relationship literally on my knees with my arms wrapped around her waist. I am embarrassed by how I tried to stop her from choosing him, her very own husband, over me. If I would have never heard the whispers of her friends, I would be an engaged man enjoying my fiancé somewhere overlooking the perfect beach. I finally faced the fact I was losing the battle of keeping her in my life and I gave her back her marriage without me. She repeatedly told me she could not continue seeing both of us. Things were too deep in our relationship, and she had to choose her marriage.

Fragile Love with Glass Affections was painful and life changing, and there are too many emotions that come with it. My homeboys have fallen victim to it over and over again from our childhood until now, but never me. The very reason I carried myself with impenetrable walls with no emotions shielded me from the pain I was experiencing. She was the first lady I ever gave my heart and Fragile Love with Glass Affections laced with deception and lies caused me to run away from the world. Her vows to another man landed me in a cabin tucked away in the woods where no one could find me.

Screaming why without an ear to hear me, I vowed to return to my old ways. Right then, I took my name out of the pot for love and the happily ever after. I do not need the house on the hill with the picketed fence protecting my son and daughter playing in the yard. Fragile Love with Glass Affections destroyed any future with my own family. My half drunken bottle of liquor and my old lifestyle waited for me to wake up whenever that was. Sleeping off the slumber I put myself in, I woke the next morning with hazy, glazed eyes and wondered exactly where I was before the ache in my heart reminded me of the recent events I wanted to forget.

* * *

I Am A Monster AND I Know It

I am a monster AND I know it!

Let me properly introduce myself. My name is Aleva, and I am five hundred and ninety-eight years old. I live wherever I choose to live for the night or week when I am not with my family. I am 5 feet and eleven inches tall with bright red hair that has not changed regardless of the decade I resurface. I am a solid one hundred and seventy pounds, and my body has curves in all the right places.

My skin is caramel chocolate, and I appeal to men and women of all races, financial standings, and statures. I have the most piercing green eyes that cannot be covered by contacts even if I tried. My lips are plump, and women pay thousands of dollars to get lips like mine. My hands, fingers, and legs are long in length resembling features of a model. To say it bluntly, I am a beautiful creature; I know it, and I use my beauty to take advantage of every situation that I enter.

My strongest weapon is I can blend in with regular humans or monsters whenever I need to. I have my parents to thank for that since my dad was an actual human and my mom was an actual monster. Becoming obsessed with her beauty and her kindness, they fell in love at fifteen years old. My mom is still one of the most beautiful creatures I have ever seen, and I inherited her looks. Poppa chose love, he chose to love Momma, and he chose to have a baby that would inherit half of him and have of a monster despite his family's failed attempts.

She has been stuck in darkness not moving on from Poppa's death. I visit her from time to time, but the energy it takes to leave her depressed world is unbearable. I must retreat into a dark cave by myself to build my energy back up before I reconnect with the rest of the world. I will not give my heart to another and risk outliving him, especially a human, even if I have many lonely nights.

My maternal grandparents taught us to love who loved us, but also to be careful not to marry a human. The time spent with them will be insignificant in the grand scheme of your life. Momma suffers every day because she went against their advice, but it did not fall on deaf ears with me. My mom has been dying slowly every day for the last five hundred and forty-three years, and the toll it has taken on everyone around her is agonizing.

My mother's family clan originated from a deep part of the world that stays undeveloped. Imagine for a second that there are caves everywhere with the most beautiful land surrounding it, and my family refuses to build it up for momentary gains. For some reason, they do not want electricity, power, or running water to disturb the simple life they have always known. We can live to be eight hundred or nine hundred years in good health, unless we are killed by the other monstrous clans, who do not have a heart for mankind or the laws of the land.

Over the years, I kept only three disassembled heads in my trophy case which belonged to my favorite archenemies: Montrose, Bitter, and Global. I never met monsters like them before, although I was warned by my paternal side of the family when Poppa made us visit them. Poppa's family were the most closed-minded people I have ever encountered, and they were prejudiced against anyone different from them. To my surprise, they were right about monsters not being trusted; and they had a level of evil in them that would destroy the goodness left in the world.

I am not sure if I was loved completely by them or if they just tolerated my mom and me. I have seen them a handful of times after Poppa died and before their deaths. The new generation of them are so unrelatable, toxic, and unfriendly that I stopped visiting them over four hundred years ago. Many of them have no idea I exist.

Fast forwarding the story along to the night I realized I was a monster and I know it, then I will backtrack to tell you about Montrose, Bitter, and Global. I was attending a private party hosted by the "It Guy" at the time, and everyone who was "anyone" was there. There was no guest list at the front door, so everyone was free to walk directly into the house and attend the party. It was strange there was no crowd control or extra security to deal with potential issues that came with large crowds.

I stayed close to the door so I could exit as quickly as possible if anything occurred. Sure enough, two hours into the party, faint cries could be heard throughout the house. At first, I could not tell if it was cries from wounded animals or wounded people, but I had to investigate before I left. Everyone else at the party did not seem to hear the cries or they may have been expecting something like this from attending one of the "It Guy's" parties before.

I walked down a flight of stairs leading to a basement, and the cries got louder. Now that the music was not blasted as loudly down here, I could hear people calling out for help through their muffled cries. I opened the door as if I was lost just to peek around the room. The monsters had locked people of different ages, colors, and sizes in glass cages, and were plucking their body parts away for pleasure. They had electrical devices attached to the cages threatening to electrocute the victims if they did not cooperate.

I counted twelve to fourteen monsters torturing these innocent people, and I had to stop this evil plan before anyone else got hurt or died. I did not have time to get to my family and return with them so we could save these people. To be honest, I liked working alone anyways. I did not want the scrutiny of how far I took things during kills. I know my mother's family would not tolerate the rage I had that was necessary living in our world sometimes.

"Think Aleva," is all I repeated to myself. I acted like I had too much to drink and stumbled in the room accidentally looking for a bathroom. They immediately put their arms around me and led me to my glass cage. I was strong enough to push my cage away from the wall, so I did not freak out like everyone else in the room. When each monster was distracted and did not notice me moving outside of my cage, I killed each of them individually. I squeezed each of them so tightly that yellow blood oozed out of their bodies as I looked them directly in their eyes.

Freeing the victims was not good enough. I ended the monsters' lives by cutting their heads off with a fingernail on my right hand. After everyone was beheaded, I put their heads in one pile, and I was proud of my handy work. I left the room to kill the "It Guy" and anyone connected to him. My new mission for the rest of my life became crystal clear that night, and it was to destroy every ugly monster causing havoc on innocent humans.

I am a monster AND I know it!

Now it is time to tell you about Montrose, Bitter, and Global. Up first is Montrose, the first monster I hated more than the ones I met before him. I was chilling and enjoying a drink inside a bar sitting off the highway. Suddenly, a greedy and cold-heartened monster entered the building, and his head would be added to my collection. Our paths crossed years before and I listened to him brag about his business adventures and how successful he was. Montrose owed the patent rights to a drug called ALMAL and he pressured people to work in his sweat factories.

This drug is very inexpensive to make, but it improved lives in remarkable ways. Certain cancers, COPD, HIV, AIDS, and Asthma show extraordinary results with complete reversals in Clinical Trials. Knowing the goldmine in his possession, Montrose continued to be the evil monster he is by overpricing the drug making it inaccessible to most of the world. He kept this miracle drug within his circle and charged the billionaires thousands of dollars per dosage.

My plan to capture Montrose had been brewing when I realized he let people die on his front yard begging for samples of ALMAL to save their lives. His love for money and power superseded his love for helping humankind. I am shocked no one took the assignment of ending this monster before me. He has been roaming the earth and getting more malicious in the last five hundred years. I had to rid the world of him and make ALMAL available for everyone.

Montrose was not a monster I could sneak up on as he would smell the plan before it was executed. He kept his inner circle small to protect himself. My plan was to lure him away from his security and the fortress he built. I heard through the grapevine that this was Montrose's favorite bar to visit when he wanted to pick up other monsters or humans for the night. I always enjoy human things as much as I can. If I needed to get my mind off the endless tasks of making the world a better place, I would go from country to country finding the right bars with the right vibe. Luckily that night, I was on a mission and enjoying myself at the same time.

There I was at the back of the bar bouncing my head to the music made by a local band. Smoke filled the room as each patron enjoyed themselves with whatever they wanted to release in the air. I smelled cigar smoke, cigarettes, marijuana, and sweet hookahs. Glasses sat on the tabletops with watered down ice as all the liquor had been sucked down. I signaled for the server to bring me another glass of my favorite poison as I tapped my feet on the floor.

There was extra commotion at the entrance doorway, and I hoped Montrose and his gang had finally arrived. Although I was enjoying myself and did not want to enter a battle, I took advantage of the opportunity laid in front of me. I watched Montrose for a good thirty minutes before I realized he liked the monster or human women to approach him to make him feel more powerful. The more beautiful they were, they were granted more time to sit at his table for drinks. Switching things up, I approached him with two drinks for the each of us, which got his attention immediately. I asked him to meet me in a free stall in the bathroom when he finished his drink.

He dismissed the other women around him and whispered he would be right back to his security. Once he arrived in the bathroom stall, I was gentle as a lamb with him. The monstrous side of me relaxed so my human side could be vulnerable. We kissed as I made it seem like it was his idea for me to remove my clothes. I took off my heels and the belt from my dress. I whispered how much it turned me on to handcuff and blindfold my partners. Montrose let me fasten the belt around his wrists behind his back as I unknowingly posed no threat to him.

I asked him to close his eyes as I removed my underwear. Being obedient to my requests and not speaking a word, he sat on the toilet. I covered his eyes with my underwear. Unexpectedly, I cut his throat from one side to the other and I watched the yellow blood ooze out by gallons. Kicking the stall door open for more room, I finished cutting off Montrose's head completely with a fingernail on my right hand. I left the bar through a backdoor with a no exit sign above it with Montrose's head for my trophy case and the key from around his neck that guarded the formula for ALMAL. Stealing the key from around his neck would not have satisfied me alone. as I would always feel incomplete if I did not take his head with me.

I am a monster AND I know it!

Up next is Bitter, the second monster I hated more than the ones I met before him. Bitter treated his citizens worse than animals were treated and he committed unthinkable crimes against them. Over a couple of years, Bitter captured all the natural resources and livestock by claiming families were not paying back taxes. With the fraudulent tax bills and limited resources, the families could not hire lawyers to fight against him. Bitter had his citizens right where he wanted them to be by forcing some families into slavery just to have meat to last throughout the winter.

Bitter eventually devalued their money, so much so, that their small savings accounts amounted to pennies. He placed himself in a position for his citizens to need him with each broken promise he made them on the campaign trail. His country got poorer and more desperate as he got richer and more violent. Bitter forcefully removed young girls from their homes to serve in his palaces. His soldiers would show up whenever they wanted and took the girls away from their families and their homes. The amount of abuse the girls endured at his hands is unbelievable as some of the girls were hassled into prostitution so his friends and he could always have fresh women to enjoy.

Many of the older girls were talked to run his day-to-day operations and they became as heartless as Bitter. They were known to kill entire families when they went out to collect taxes that were due when the families did not have the money. As some of the girls aged, they begin to teach Bitter's ways to the next generation of girls. It was either they passed down the hatred for mankind or got stoned to death in front of the entire palace. Many of them were dishonoring their families, but that betrayal was not as strong as the willingness to live.

I could not sit back and watch innocent people be tortured or degraded so Bitter could feel more dominant. A party was thrown at the Royal Palace, and I decided to make my move on that perfect occasion. There would not be much resistance as heaps of alcohol were served to Bitter's guests. I hung out in the darkness until the last guest drifted off to sleep and the sleeping quarters were free of the young girls. I set the entire sleeping quarters on fire where Bitter and his friends were sleeping, and no one could escape the impenetrable barrier I placed on the doors, windows, and ceiling. No one could go in and no one could come out.

Bitter and his friends were facing an easy death as I felt like they deserved more from the pain people suffered under their enjoyment. Burnt skin could be smelled for miles away and the fire burned for hours. I entered the other side of Bitter's palace where the girls' living quarters were. The fire had not spread there yet, and I wanted to escort the girls safely out. The older girls found weapons to fight me as they felt like it was a setup leading them to death. Conquering them all in the mini battles without hurting them too much, I offered the route the others had taken. Many of them felt like Bitter or his security would be on the outside of the palace with guns to teach them another lesson.

As soon as I led them safely outside the palace, I went back for unfinished business. I found Bitter in the sleeping quarters trying to climb out of a window as many of the other guests were dead from the fire or smoke. I squeezed Bitter's neck until the yellow liquid poured from his eyes, nose, mouth, and ears. I cut his head off with a fingernail on my right hand. Sticking to my old habits, I cut off the heads of all his guests and placed them in a pile. Victoriously, the girls and I rode off into the sunset as if nothing happened, and I had Bitter's head to place in my trophy case.

I am a monster AND I know it!

I had the displeasure of meeting Global at an All-Star NBA basketball game. He was the most deceitful monster I ever encountered, and I felt his negative energy as soon as our hands touched during the introduction. His name probably was not Global and everything about him was questionable. He loved deskinning humans and displaying their skin in open markets around town as part of his monthly rituals. He allowed everyone in his events as he wanted to use his victims as examples to keep others in line. Global had great taste as he decorated the market in the finest décor and served the best meals to his guest. The setup was too expensive and too nice to be in the back alley of the market.

Some of the richest monsters and humans flew in from all over the world to be a part of Global's annual events. Attaching their names to Global's name was a game changer for them instead of the negative connotation it should have carried. My flirtation and ability to read a person worked in my favor as I received my golden invitation in the mail to attend Global's annual event at his mansion. The invitation mentioned our brief meeting at the All-Star NBA basketball game, and he hoped he could get to know me better. Perfect! I was going to end Global's life that night. I unsuccessfully tried to get in his mansion before, but it was guarded tightly with the best security money could buy.

The night of Global's annual event, I did not know what to expect but I stayed as alert as possible to everyone and everything. My nerves were as hard as steel. This monster had to die, and I am sure this annual event was going to put his monthly rituals at the open market to shame. No phones, cameras, or recording devices were allowed during the events, and all guests had to sign a non-disclosure agreement before entering. No one outside of Global's previous guest list knew the layout inside of his mansion. Since I could not properly plan by getting the blueprint, I had to figure out who was security the night of the event and it was too many of them for me to fight by myself.

Even though my Momma's clan is known for being the strongest clan of monsters to exist, the recovery time to rebuild after huge fights is what is so bothersome. I was planning to do the least amount of fighting to kill Global. I walked undetectably throughout his mansion and set fires in a couple of the rooms that guests were not occupying. Everyone exited the mansion in an unorderly fashion and trampled over each other trying to get to safety.

While he was on the phone, I quietly walked behind Global and blew the Breath of Death in his face. Only ten monsters in the world were gifted with the Breath of Death and I only used it when necessary. Momma's family clan kept my gift a secret so I would not become a target by other monsters. I did not wait to see Global's body drop. I needed to hide before his security figured out it was me. I heard them yelling Master as they all ran to him to see why he was lying still and not responding. Several of them attending to his body as head of security told the rest of them to secure the mansion.

Whatever was inside of the mansion was more important to security than searching the ground outside where everyone was. Figuring out what happened to Global should have been top priority. I slowly headed back to the mansion as I questioned what I was going to find as I searched. I made it to the second level of the mansion without being detected as I tapped on walls to find hidden hallways or rooms. Nothing was found but I could not let the feeling go that something was not right. Suddenly, I spotted a man dressed in an expensive gray suit and I wrinkled my nose wondering where he came.

The carpet was not as evenly spread as it was when I came through earlier. There is no way a secret room could be under the second floor of the mansion without me being able to find it on the first floor. I began to tap my feet all around the misplaced carpet until I felt uneven flooring. I lifted the carpet to see glass instead of wood which covered the flooring over the entire mansion. I slid the glass back until it revealed a ladder attached to a wall that led me to a dark room underneath the second floor. A hint of light could be seen through the darkness and the quietness was unnerving, but I could not leave. Global was hiding something!

I walked until I heard the first sound under the glass entry way. Fifteen people were chained and gagged but it was too dark for me to see who they were. Rushing to free them, one of them begged me to leave him alone. He would rather face his death at Global's mansion than to have his skin displayed at the open market for the entire town to see. He did not want to bring shame to his family by appearing weak. I explained to him that Global would not be a problem for anyone anymore and I would get them out of this situation. I was not leaving the mansion with anyone breathing but the fifteen people who I was getting ready to rescue.

As I freed three of them, I heard chattering coming towards us. The victims started to freak out as I told them to go back to their respective spots and pretend to be bound. I reassured them as much as I could that they were safe if I was with them. The men did not come all the way down the hall where we were. There was another hallway on the left that they walked down that I did not see when I was walking that way.

The nervous one in the group started telling me that Global was as controlling and powerful as he was since everyone feared him. He often threatened other influential men in town by capturing them and skinning them alive in front of their families. The prominent men in town did exactly what Global wanted them to do. Another one spoke up to say that Global had planned to skin them alive in front of the guest tonight as a warning. I faced all the victims and told them that Global was dead already and he died at my hands. I promised to take out security before leading them to safety and I needed them to stay in the room looking like they were still detained.

Global's security and staff were mourning his death and verbally complaining that their status in town would not be the same without him. I exited the room the same way I entered through the glass sliding door and took out Global's people one by one. I checked the front lawn to make sure I did not leave anyone alive before returning to the hidden room with the victims. The victims were shaking and scared as I begged them to come with me immediately. I could not predict that Global had other hired people not at the event and it was imperative that we started to move.

Holding their hands and guiding them slowly towards the ladder was progress. Many of them were frozen in place. I hid the victims in a room that was locked during the party once everyone was on the second floor. I wanted to survey the mansion one last time to confirm we were safe to leave. Rushing back to the room to gather them, I stressed again we needed to move speedily and quietly to our cars. Each of them listened to me as we sprinted out the front door to our cars. Safe at last, many of them sped down the street like maniacs.

Global's body still laid in his front yard, and I killed everyone that should have been guarding it. He was the easiest kill I've had in a long time. Most monsters give up more fight to save their lives. After all, he did not see me coming or that I had the Breath of Death that would end his life. Being as I did not use all my energy fighting, I am grateful that it will not take days to recover from this kill.

I approached Global's body carefully to make sure no extra security or staff arrived to guard it. The last time I checked the ground, it was clear and no one was alive on the land but me. I grabbed Global and cut off his head with a fingernail on my right hand. I went back in the mansion and found all the dead people that were previously killed by me to cut off their heads too. I placed their heads in a pile on Global's front lawn as I grabbed Global's head as my keepsake.

I am a monster AND I know it!

* * *

Small Town Love Affair

Kernel Theodore Greyson watched from the tiny window in his garage at the excitement happening next door as he sharpened his knives. His knife collection was one of his proudest possessions, and he never left it behind regardless of where life's journey took him. As each blade stroked the worn leather strap, Kernel Greyson's internal battle heightened to an unhealthy level. He could not trust himself, nor liked himself, when his agitation rose to great high. His happy pill meant to calm him down did not always work as fast as he needed it to work.

Oblivious to his feelings, the laughter ranged loudly from the children reminding him of his own kids he lost during his personal custody battle. It was as if his family disappeared off the face of the earth, without him doing anything to aid in their disappearance. Kernel Greyson had a reputation in the woods with his fellow soldiers for "making things disappear" without a trace, and no one outside of a military uniform knew the depth of this secret. Adjusting to society after thirty years of serving was difficult at times. A lot of situations triggered his PTSD, and he was too stubborn to get the professional help he needed. Every now and then, he indulged in the warfare raging in his mind, and it always resulted in loneliness and regret.

The loud thud of a ball hitting Kernel Greyson's garage door brought him out of his trance, in which he was daydreaming of a future with his family that would never happen again. His behavior towards his wife secured a life without her. His overly aggressive tactics scared her and had the opposite effect on the way he wanted things to be. He closed his eyes to hold back the raw emotions building inside of him and hoped the fresh tears would not flow from his eyes. Frustrated for not screaming at the neighborhood kids for being in his yard, he blamed himself for their toys touching any part of his property.

Kernel Greyson was far from the meek and mild neighbor he pretended to be. He had seething thoughts of how to keep them all in line and he hoped one day he would not act upon them. Distracted from the task at hand, Kernel Greyson stropped the knives more than the recommended five to seven strokes per side. Metal particles from the knife sharpening process were piled on the floor causing more cleanup work for Kernel Greyson. On a day like today, he usually welcomed the unnecessary tasks and additional chores to prevent him from doing God knows what to innocent people.

Nothing seemed to calm the beast within, and he was now on the battlefield with the enemy fifty feet away from him and his military unit surrounded. He chose to replay the next ten minutes, which often felt like ten years, as he slain more men than humanly possible. His techniques were unnatural, and he would be a rich man if he could bottle up his methods for profit. The noise from the neighborhood frightened him and brought him out of his trance.

Sirens could be heard outside of Kernel Greyson's neighborhood and a lot of traffic could be seen heading briskly down the highway. Everyone assumed it was due to the body that was found seven miles south on Highway 46 in a dingy hotel. The body was so badly dismantled, the police was unsure of the gender or age of the victim upon arrival. The crime scene was described as one from a horror movie with blood dripping from the ceiling and doorknobs. The carpet was stained beyond repair and body parts were scattered around the tiny hotel room from the front door to the bathroom bathtub.

The cheap furniture could not withstand the pressure of the events as most of it was destroyed or drenched in blood. Kernel Greyson's entire neighborhood was on alert and the trees surrounding their properties were not a solid plan of defense against a killer of this magnitude. Whispers among the neighbors and the fright on the kids' faces became the reason the Neighborhood Watch started its nightly patrols again.

Small towns, like the one he currently lived in, worked best for Kernel Greyson as it was easier to remain a stranger. He did not need extra attention on him. He learned the culture of each small town and mimic the behavior enough to stay safely under the radar. The PTSD therapy he received when he arrived back in The States highly suggested he seek such living arrangements. They tend to be quieter, and he would be able to reestablish himself in society more successfully. The techniques taught in the sessions did little to no good for his mental health as he was not opened to doing the necessary work.

He began to lose everything and everybody that meant something to him, and he cursed all the training and all the people who would try to help someone like him. Kernel

Greyson was up at night twirling one of his knives pondering how easy it was to peel flesh off someone's bones with the tip of the knife. He had to control the impulses. He did not want to start over in another small town identical to the town he lived now. Moving so much under different aliases might catch up to him some day.

The neighborhood Kernel Greyson settled in this time was a family orientated neighborhood with little to no outside traffic. This neighborhood was tucked neatly in the suburbs with families of all nationalities and backgrounds living harmoniously together. A neighborhood church was beyond the gates of the secured neighborhood and the pastor of the church lived within the confined community too. Pastor Bentley Williams was always available for wherever his flock needed him. The kids in the neighborhood went to the same schools and played recreational sports together in the evenings. Moms carpooled to their events together and Dads went hiking or hunting as a group. The only exception to the "perfect neighborhood" was the gruesome unsolved murder seven miles away.

The news of a body being found in the small town caught national attention and the heat was turned up on finding out who could have committed such a crime in this "picture-perfect" neighborhood. The police now gathered the body, which was proclaimed to be a young girl, named Venus Manhattan, who attended the local university from the remaining DNA in the room. Venus was twenty-two years old and was a Political Science major with hopes of graduating in the spring with the next graduating class. She worked at the local bar downtown a couple nights each week and appeared to be handling the responsibility of school and her job well.

Venus was from a large city and had difficulties fitting in the small town in the beginning. Lack of discipline with her grades, irresponsibility with partying, and hanging out too much limited her choices of where she could further her education. Since The University in this small town was the only one to accept her, Venus packed her bags five years ago and moved thousands of miles away from her family and friends. She hoped the small town would settle her wild ways, and she hoped she would become more responsible.

Finding out about her death, Venus' roommate, Voilet, was careful not to move any of her things. Her roommate had seen several police shows on tv and comprehended that clues could be hiding in plain sight. The police found Venus' diary among her things in her dorm room in the bottom dresser drawer with papers hiding its location. Venus was a very detailed person and wrote everything down in her diary or on her personal calendar to stay organized. Her diary held all her secret cravings for more adventure to spice up her life so she could erase the pain her heart often felt from the bad choices she made.

The lead detective assigned to her case, Detective Antonio Williams known as "Guts" in the department, planned to read her diary and calendar to cross reference it with her classes and work schedule. Her diary revealed details that she hid under initials or emojis which reoccurred in both. Venus' yearning for an adventure went far beyond an amusement ride or a road trip as she stated in her diary. She described a secret life in detail that her best friend, who was her sister, did not know existed.

The police were unable to pinpoint a timeline of her disappearance because Venus had isolated herself from the people she had become to love and spent her free time. She was last seen at the local coffee shop with her roommate about two days before her murder and her roommate reported she was very distance and defensive during most of the conversation. Venus had recently broken up with her boyfriend without an explanation other than she needed space, and the relationship was not working for her anymore. Venus said to anyone who would listen to her that she was ready for graduation so she could get on with more important things in her life.

Kernel Greyson was never terrified, or worried that any harm would come to him. His military background and martial art training prepared him. He had become a legal weapon with his hands and that much more dangerous if he had a gun or his favorite weapon, knives, in them. He kept his knives always sharpened and his guns cleaned. He was ready to protect himself from another tragedy like the one that occurred on Highway 46. Until the police crack the case, Kernel Greyson was on high alert and hoped paranoia does not seep through his skin when he encounters other people. He successfully escaped the questions from the police one evening as he left the grocery store near the hotel where the body was found.

Cars were being pulled over matching the description the eyewitnesses gave in connection to the murder. He was unaware the police had a car connected to the crime. He did not hear those details on the news or on his personal police scanner he kept in his garage. However, Kernel Greyson answered the questions satisfactorily for the rookie cops, who were sent to secure the roads leading into and out of the small town. No doubt he was going to remain safe and out of prison.

The body was found five days before and the police did not have any solid leads other than the killer was probably a professional, and the crime was not committed in an act of rage. According to Detective Williams, the crime scene was left in such disarray that it intended to throw the investigation off or lead the police down the wrong path. The only fingerprints found in the entire room under the bloody clutter was Venus' and one of the housekeepers. All the blood and hair in the room belonged to Venus only. The cameras surrounding the hotel were all malfunctioning and offered no evidence to the police.

Although this town was known for its neighborly love and safety, a dark side did exist with a bar, a strip club, and a questionable massage parlor in a part of town most people chose to ignore. The upstanding citizens visited this side of town late at night and had guarantees that their reputation would not be tarnished, or their comings and goings would be discovered. They pulled their wealth together to disable cameras, reroute 911 calls, and paid the business owners well to keep their mouths shut and their secrets protected.

Pastor Williams sensed the rising concern and tension, so he organized prayer meetings for the citizens in his neighborhood and surrounding neighborhoods. Everyone was welcomed to come. At first, the crowds showed up in great numbers because they were all concerned about the safety of their own families. As the weeks went by, the crowds got smaller and smaller, and the talk of the murdered college girl, named Venus Manhattan, was talked about less and less.

Life seemed to be returning to normal and all immediate threats seemed to have disappeared. The police exhausted all their leads and interviewed countless residents on what they saw that might be of any significance. Pastor Williams continued to pound the pavement each day praying over the safety of his church members and for justice to be served. One life lost to a senseless murder was too much for him to roll over and sleep peacefully at night.

Meanwhile, Venus' family arrived in the small town to assist the police in solving her crime. They hoped that Venus' family would shed more details about her to aid in the investigation. The police had not shared too much of the details in Venus' diary with them over the phone and Detective Williams promised to do so in person. He met the family at the airport and extended his condolences to each of them individually. He explained to the family the manpower already used to solve Venus' case and the endless pursuit of justice would continue to be served.

Venus' younger sister, named Eva, was confident she could help once she read the diary. She identified with her sister better than anyone and they had an unbreakable bond, and they shared most of their secrets with each other. Eva remembered nights Venus would go missing and would not call her back for days with no explanation as to where she had been other than school and work, which was taking up a lot of her time. Eva had an uneasy feeling that her sister's disappearances had something to do with the hidden details of her murder.

Pastor Williams mentioned the need for extra help for the Neighborhood Watch Patrol to Kernel Greyson at the grocery store one evening as they were checking out their grocery at the same time. Kernel Greyson was hesitant at first to sign up. He wanted to stay completely away from anyone in authority in town. However, he was very curious the information Pastor Williams was privy since his eldest son was assigned to the case of the murder college girl, Venus Manhattan. Pastor Williams felled right into the trap set for him by overly sharing a bloody shoe print was found at the back of the hotel and the suspected killer wore a size twelve shoe.

The police were waiting on a couple of the manufacturing companies to share their buyers' information. The boot was an exclusive hiking brand not sold worldwide and issued by the military only. Pastor Williams told Kernel Greyson a boot was the only solid lead after combing through the evidence for months. Detective Williams decided not to share this information with the local or national media as it was the only connection to the killer that seemed conclusive. Kernel Greyson made a mental note to destroy his military issued size twelve hiking boots as soon as he could.

The University held several candlelight vigils in Venus' honor once her family arrived, and they were opened to the press being on campus anytime they chose to be there. The University wanted to convey the message to their current students and family members that the school was safe and so was the town in which the school was built. It had a rich history, and the alumni felt honored to have received the education they received from The University.

During the difficult months, the alumni often showed up to help hang flyers for Venus and aid the town in any way they could. With the tight security around the town, the campus, and in Kernel Greyson's neighborhood; one could often wonder how a crime of such magnitude could happen right under their noses.

One rainy Friday morning in November, the list arrived at the Police Department with the names of people who purchased a size twelve military issued boot from the manufacturing company matching the footprint at the crime scene. The list was not of much help, as it had seemed random at best, as none of its citizens were listed except Pastor Williams. The police sergeant mentioned the names on the list during that morning's briefing but did not assign anyone to follow up on the list. Detective Williams could not let go of the feeling that Kernel Greyson's address was on the list but under a different name and ruled it as no coincidence.

He looked personally into Kernel Greyson's background as the case emerged from the dark side of town. However, he overlooked his dad's name, as his dad was the neighborhood pastor, and he served his country honorably. On the other hand, the entire town did not associate with Kernel Greyson. His personality and his military background scared them a little. He had the ability to commit such a crime based on those facts alone.

As soon as the sergeant dismissed the detectives and police officers, Detective Williams decided he was going to pay Kernel Greyson a visit to feel him out. He wanted the visit to be one that completely took Kernel Greyson by surprised so he would not have a chance to cover his tracks or come up with a believable alibi. Choosing one of the unmarked police cars, Detective Williams was on his way to Kernel Greyson to question his whereabouts on the night Venus Manhattan was killed. Being an eager young detective, Detective Williams made a rookie mistake by not calling his suspicious trip to his fellow comrades.

Kernel Greyson and Pastor Williams were in the woods running a couple of miles together that morning. They bonded so well during the Neighborhood Watch Patrol coverage and began to hang out on a regular basis. Their conversations remained light as they ran up and down the different terrains and trails. Pastor Williams expressed his gratitude to Kernel Greyson for his assistance again and how inviting it was to have a former military family member ready and willing to assist. Kernel Greyson silently expressed his gratitude. He was able to destroy his boots the same night he arrived home. He burned the boots in his garage in a fireproof barrel and took the remaining ashes to a dump site before the sun rose the next morning.

Kernel Greyson had not returned home from his run with Pastor Williams by the time Detective Williams arrived at his home. Kernel Greyson often left his side door to the garage opened when he went on runs so he would not have to take keys with him. No one has ever evaded his privacy when he was not home. His neighbors never felt a need to visit him nor was they crazy enough to invade his home when he was not there. Detective Williams knocked on the front door and the garage door announcing his reasoning for being there.

Once he did not get an answer, he decided to peep through a window that was eye level to observe the objects stored in the garage. Detective Williams turned all the doorknobs hoping one of them was not locked. Just his luck, the garage door was open. As he entered the side door of the garage, he was extremely excited he had gained access inside Kernel Greyson's home, and he needed to be in and out within a couple of minutes. Not finding anything suspicious in the house, Detective Williams was almost done looking around in the garage. However, something shiny caught his attention in the corner of the garage.

It was a thick black case about 12 x 9 x 4 in dimension with patented latches. Detective Williams confidently recognized its contents were professional knives. His uncle had a similar case he kept hidden in his basement when he was a kid. As soon as Detective Williams finished examining the knives held within the case, he grabbed his radio to request backup at Kernel Greyson's home. Venus' killer used specialty knives, which left distinctive patterns on her body. Detective Williams was sure these knives could have done the kind of damage found on Venus' body and had the ability to partially disassembled it also.

There was no way Detective Williams was going to wait on a search warrant as he started taking pictures of the evidence. He was more than convinced Kernel Greyson was the killer and was planning to bring him in for questioning as soon as he arrived back home. These knives are exactly the pieces of evidence Detective Williams needed to close Venus' case. Out of nowhere, Kernel Greyson opened the garage door to find Detective Williams taking photos and speaking into a voice recorder.

He asked the detective if he had lost his mind and figured out a way to escape from the garage and out of town. Feeling cornered, Kernel Greyson launched for Detective Williams knocking his voice recorder and gun out of his hands. He ran towards the woods leaving his car in the driveway with Detective Williams running behind him. Kernel Greyson was in top notch shape to be as old as he was, and Detective Williams would not be able to catch him on his best day.

On the other side of town, Eva read her sister's diary, and she was excited to figure out her sister's secret. Venus had a new lover, who was much older than she was, and he was well respected in town. He had a family and appeared to be happily married with no plans to leave home. Venus described the excitement of dating a powerful, married man in the small town with no one knowing their secret and how the affair gave her the desired amount of adventure she craved.

She expressed how school and the relationship with her ex-boyfriend was trivial and how she envisioned a more satisfying life with her new lover. The affair was wrong, but

Venus was not strong enough to end it, nor did she want to end it. After an argument with her new lover ignoring her when he came into the bar, Venus threatened to cut things off with him as a game to make him want her more. He insisted he would leave his family for her if that was what it took for Venus not to leave him.

Venus documented the day she and her new lover got matching tattoos as a commitment to one another. Eva could not figure out what the diamond, sunrays, pyramid, and the V and B initials meant other than the "B" was her new lover's name. Venus said the location was on their right rib hidden out of sight to protect their privacy and to bond them that much closer together.

Eva went to the local coffee shop for a breather and to see what the hype was about this small town that her sister could not stop talking about once she was accepted into The University. She watched people come and go and prayed for more clues to help solve her sister's murder. She could not figure out who the "B" was in her diary and she knew that was the secret to cracking her sister's case.

A nice-looking man came into the coffee shop and seemed to be loved by everyone. He slowly made his way over to Eva as she stood out like a sore thumb. Knowing everyone in town, he did not recognize her and concluded she must be Venus' sister. He wanted to properly introduce himself as Pastor Bentley Williams and he was the pastor of the only church in the small town. He shared with Eva that Detective Williams was his son and there were no new details in Venus' case.

As the pastor of the small town, he felt it was his duty to meet Venus' family and pray for them. Before Pastor Williams could sit down at Eva's table, he knocked over the chair at the next table as his foot got tangled under the table next to Eva. He was saying good morning to other residents of the small town and was not paying full attention to what he was doing. Pastor Williams was a little nervous about meeting Venus' family. He felt partially responsible for her death due to his not covering the town more effectively with prayers.

He told Eva her sister had one of the kindest spirits of anyone he has ever met, and it was a pleasure getting to know her through the Lord's work she did at the church. Eva was quite shocked by his comment as Venus had an issue with organized religion and vowed to never participate in it. Eva thanked him for coming over to introduce himself and she shared her optimism with Pastor Williams about finding the killer as she pushed her chair from the table.

Suddenly, Eva did not feel the warm, fuzzy feeling from Pastor Williams as all the other patrons in the coffee shop did. Maybe it was the sharpness of the tone he used with her or the "pastor voice" in which he spoke making himself seem more important than anyone else in there. He gave her the creeps and she wanted to get far away from him so she could dive back into Venus' diary a second time. She was sure she missed other significant clues that Venus left behind.

As she rounded the corner of the Coffee Shop, Pastor Williams was dead in her tracks. He grabbed her arm roughly and told her they needed to talk more privately. Eva brushed his hand off her arm spilling the remainder of her coffee down her leg. She glanced down briefly, and he was wearing boots like the police said the killer was wearing. Not knowing a lot about hiking boots, Eva could have been grasping at straws out of desperation. Why else would Pastor Williams be grabbing on her and demanding they talk more privately, unless he knows more than he said in the coffee shop?

The "B" stood for Bentley and PASTOR BENTLEY WILLIAMS WAS MY SISTER'S LOVER AND KILLER! As if on cue, a police cruiser pulled up behind Eva and Pastor Williams. Eva was scared out of her mind and did not know what her next move was going to be. The Police Sergeant exited the car and walked straight towards them. He expressed his gratitude to Pastor Williams for his vigilance in finding the town's killer and acknowledged his appreciation in welcoming Venus' family into town. Eva ran as fast as she could away from Pastor Williams as she did not want to be the next victim in this small town.

Once she felt she was a safe distance from Pastor Williams, she called a shared car to head back to her sister's dorm room. Now more than ever, she needed to reread the diary, calm herself down, and figure out Pastor Williams' part in her sister's murder and cover up. Rumors of Kernel Greyson abruptly leaving town floated faster than the deer in the woods sprinting to not be killed. He became the small town's only suspect and the news media had been called to give an update to the public.

Detective Williams was going to release details about Venus' murder that had not been mentioned to the public. Everyone needed to be on the lookout for Kernel Greyson and understand how dangerous he was. Fighting through the headache and his throbbing left eye from the blow Kerner Greyson gave him, he called his dad to update him and express his frustration. Pastor Williams answered the phone very flustered, but he wanted to know the latest details of Venus' case. He told his dad that the killer seemed to be two steps ahead of them during the entire investigation until now.

One of the eyewitnesses mentioned a man about six feet tall and weighing two hundred and fifteen pounds leaving the crime scene on the night Venus was murdered. He wore black clothes and ran towards the woods near the hotel. Kernel Greyson fit that description as well as forty percent of the men living in the small town. So did Pastor Williams, but he was never considered amongst the guilty. His son being the lead detective and the title he held at the church excluded him from becoming a suspect.

Reading her sister's diary took precedence over everything once she arrived at the dorm. She locked the door and decided to put on the news for background noise. As she sat on the bed, a news break came on the tv interrupting the scheduled show. She found the remote control and turned the volume up. She wanted to know what was so important that needed to be shared with the world before the 6:00 pm evening news. Since Detective Williams had not called her family first about Venus' case, she relaxed on the side of the bed waiting for the announcement.

Reaching for her water bottle to take a sip, Eva read the caption incorrectly on the tv. The police department was getting ready to report the solved murder of college girl, Venus Manhattan, which occurred months ago. Tears flowed down Eva's face as she sensed something was not right about this entire news coverage. Panic and fright were all Eva felt as her parents arrived in Venus' dorm room. They were going to hear the unfortunate news together as a family.

Eva screamed "no" as loud as she could, and her parents alleged the stress of Venus' murder had finally gotten to her. Falling to the floor and grabbing her head, Eva believed with every fiber of her being that the killer was not Kernel Theodore Greyson but Pastor Bentley Williams. The time for her to tell her parents what Venus had been hiding, why Venus was killed, and she knows the police has the wrong guy in custody was at that moment. Eva was so sure Pastor Williams was the killer that she would have bet a million dollars on it and her family did not have that kind of money.

Eva researched Pastor Williams as soon as she finished reading the diary and he has a tattoo on his right rib that matched the one Venus described in her diary. A recent picture from a hiking trip for the youth showed Pastor Williams without a shirt on by the time they reach the peak of the mountain. She could clearly see a tattoo with a diamond, sunrays, a pyramid, and the L and B initials. He captioned the picture on social media that he needed to be the first to the top this time. The last time his youth group made him shave his head and eyebrows off when he came in last place.

Pastor Williams' lack of hair would explain why his DNA was not found in the room. Eva's plans were to build her case, present it to her family, and find an unbiased person at the police station to listen to her. As she waited to speak with a detective, Pastor Williams came through the side entrance of the police station as if he wore a badge himself. Not able to contain herself, she started to scream to the top of her lungs that Pastor Williams killed her sister, and he was a dirty scoundrel. Before Eva could reach Pastor Williams, a swarm of cops of all ranks were standing in between them.

The police sergeant quickly escorted the family to a private room which was supposed to be a safe space. She shared her findings and who she thought the killer was. The police sergeant had a scripted response to all of Eva's reasons. He encouraged the family to leave town until the pending trial started and he would keep them updated on any new evidence in the case. Detective Williams told Eva he understood her pain but accusations like that was not going to be tolerated in their small town. He further explained that the evidence pointed to Kernel Greyson, and they would not stop searching for him until they had him in custody.

Eva's biggest fear had come true as the police sergeant explained that a lot of young girls have an unhealthy obsession with Pastor Williams. His status in town, his good looks, and his kindness attracted unnecessary attention. Pastor Williams had a way of making everybody feel at home and like the most important person in the world. He further explained his fourteen-year marriage and his devotion to his wife and kids were admired by other married people in town. Eva left out of the police station with tears streaming from her eyes and Pastor Williams unfortunately won that round. This was not the last this small town would hear from Eva Manhattan, and she promised they could mark her word.

Chapter III:

Finding Redemption

* * *

A Redemption Story

Sweat ran down Matt's face as he heard the doorknob jingling on the other side of the door as he entered the password in the safe. Only seconds remained to replace the stolen money before being hauled off to jail without a possibility of parole, or worst, killed! The room was dark, and it felt hotter than a mid-day in the desert. Matt swore he would never get into trouble again if God delivered him from his own mess once more.

He had been raised by good parents with solid values, but Matt's desire for a fast lifestyle repeatedly landed him in such situations. As the door swung open, Matt hid behind the shower curtain in the bathroom attached to the Bail Bondmen's office. He heard both partners swearing and promising to break every bone in his body if he betrayed them

100

as they believed he had. Matt had indeed done all the things they accused him of doing such as stealing their money, impersonating a Bail Bondman, lying about his background, and selling their guns on the black market to the highest bidder.

With his large football frame, likable personality, and good-looking face, Matt never had a problem convincing people that he was who he pretended to be. The truth was, Matt was a con artist with impeccable social skills who would deceive anyone to get what he wanted. Trying to figure out how he had been one step ahead of them, Matt heard the Bail Bondmen close the doors minutes later. Slowly stepping out of the shower, he exercised extreme caution, knowing he could not be anywhere near the building, or he would be in danger.

Glancing down the hallway for anyone except the cleaning crew, Matt rushed to the stairwell. Ten flights of stairs did not deter him. It felt like a matter of life or death to get away undetected. Reaching the bottom step on the first floor, he was out of breath and his clothes were drenched with sweat. Still not out of the woods, Matt had to make it safely to his rental car parked blocks away. Security wished Matt a good night as he hastily passed their desk. Matt tipped his head as he had no words left to speak due to exhaustion.

Slapping his skin sharply, the cold night air was refreshening as Matt's body temperature boiled from the intensity of getting away safely. The end of the block seemed miles away and he had to walk it normally to avoid drawing attention to himself. Finally, he could see his getaway car three blocks down the road and sprinted the rest of the way. As he sat in the car, Matt removed his coat and hat, which felt suffocating, and he was having a hard time breathing. The windows instantly fogged up from the heat escaping from Matt's body.

On the ride to his new apartment, Matt relished the rush of getting away with his crimes. The deceit made him feel powerful and untouchable. He was not able to hold down solid relationships with women or anyone for that matter, and he was often lonely until he met his next companion. He was thankful for the cute little lady he met last week at the gas station around the corner from his old apartment. Maybe, just maybe, she was willing to spend the rest of the night with him and take his mind off the last couple of hours. First, Matt had to get out of the damp clothes, shower, and figure out what he was going to eat.

Hours later, the fireplace and candles were lit as soft music played in the background of Matt's perfect bachelor's pad. It was located downtown, hidden amongst the taller buildings and busy people. His apartment had the best view, an open floor plan, and a huge balcony large enough to host a party. Matt stocked his bar with premium liquor, beer, and wine and no one should want anything to drink outside of his collection. The refrigerator was fully loaded with finger foods due to the fact he was a man who could not cook, nor desired to learn how. If any of his guests needed anything outside of what he had available, they would have to wait until they left his apartment to be satisfied.

Matt's guest arrived on time, which was typical for the type of women he liked to get involved. As one could guess, he had a certain type of woman he dated, and her looks, body, hair, her confidence, her independence, clothing, purses, and the type of car she drove fit the profile of someone living Matt's life. There was never a commitment made to them beyond that night and no promises were given for a future. Matt was crystal clear to avoid drama, feelings, and misunderstandings with his lady friends. Besides, he trusted only his parents and his siblings, who could not rely on anything Matt said or did.

Waking up feeling reinvigorated the next morning, Matt's mission for the day was to find another hustle that was going to pay for his lifestyle. It was not going to be an honest gig because that is not what he did. The faster the hustle and payout, the more attracted Matt became. He was not above cheating and lying to anyone, even the elderly and children. One of Matt's most successful fraudulent schemes was being the President of a non-profit organization raising money to assist children. He was surprised how the wealthy was willing to invest in the future of children they cared nothing about other than a tax write-off. A fake letterhead with an EIN number, a custom shirt, a briefcase, and a bank account were all he invested to raise millions of dollars.

Matt's expensive taste rarely allowed him to save some of the money he scammed from folks. Once he had a nice nest egg, he began to travel abroad for months at a time and ate at the finest restaurants. He bought new cars, suits, furniture, and jewelry to impress the upper class, which were his victims. Many of them did not see the setup from the start as Matt's fake business was always in their field of expertise. Holding a master's degree in business, he could rub elbows with the best of them with his smooth talk. He had businessmen and businesswomen eating out of the palm of his hand until he executed his plan to rob them blind.

A CFO's job posting at a major stock company caught Matt's eye as they were replacing their current CFO, who was retiring. Confident he could play the role of a CFO, he cleared his throat and picked up his phone. He told the CFO's secretary he would have his assistant submit his resume and call next week to schedule a sit-down interview. By the time Matt hung up the phone, the secretary was promising she would use all her power to ensure he was one of the final candidates. Matt made a note on his notepad to send his resume from his fictitious assistant with his fabricated resume. Meanwhile, he pulled up the last resume he used in Corporate America and tweaked the job descriptions to match the job requirements.

Matt was tired and looking forward to the downtime between his scams. He was going to one of his family's Sunday Dinners and at least try to make peace with his family. Loving them more than anything, besides himself, Matt did not like the rift between them. He lied about what he was doing now, who he was dating, when he was going to bring her to dinner, and pledged he would attend church with the family soon. He really missed each of them for the way they loved him and the special bond he used to share with them.

One of his aliases faked his way through the interview, and Matt started the job sooner than he expected. Knowing the company's private information he would be exposed, he agreed to working part-time immediately. He still had to work out his pretend notice at his previous phony job. He had not planned to be around long enough for his full-time employment to begin or his previous phony job to end. He would have keys to unlock every door of the kingdom sooner than later. Matt was planning to rush in, steal more money than he cared to count, experience a bogus family emergency, and lay low until his money was almost gone.

Just like he planned, Matt sat on the beach, enjoying the view and the beautiful people three and a half weeks after becoming the CFO. His wife and kids were involved in a devastating accident, and they remained in critical condition. He had to be by their bedsides. Not wanting to see him depart the company, HR, in a show of surprising support, had allowed Matt to use FMLA to retain his benefits, to ensure his family received proper care. Gullible fools ran through Matt's mind in the HR office as he cried his eyes out. Noticing a family walking by with a mom, a dad, one daughter, and two sons, Matt became homesick and went to his parents' house after vacation.

Matt stood outside of his parents' house for a few minutes, unsure whether it was okay to use his key or ring the doorbell like a stranger. One of the elder neighbors called to him from across the street. He walked over to her house to speak and hugged her. Turning around to head back across the street, the fence to the backyard was now open. He froze in place contemplating whether he should go in the backyard or solve the dilemma he had before the elder neighbor summoned him, use his key or ring the doorbell like a stranger. His mom ended all debates by walking out of the gate, and he felt like he was eight years old seeing her again.

Surrounded by his entire family for dinner on his parents' deck, Matt was unusually quiet and noticeably uncomfortable. The familiar skeptical questions were coming from his siblings and the same hurtful disappointment would rest on his parents' faces. He was ready to get it over with so he could enjoy the night's air with a nice drink and cigar before heading to bed. Instead of the questions and stares, everyone acted as if Matt was not there and carried on naturally. No one mentioned his lifestyle or barely addressed him at dinner, which hurt a lot more than the stares or questions ever did. Coming home was a mistake and he considered leaving first thing in the morning.

Matt remained in his childhood bedroom later than he planned Sunday morning. Not knowing if he wanted to stay at his parents' house, he deliberated whether he was going to church. He could go running, have coffee, and run a few more errands before the family came back home. However, the house rule was anyone who stayed there on a Saturday night went to church with the family on Sunday morning. Shaking off the hesitation, he headed to the shower to get ready for church. He wanted to head downstairs a little earlier than the rest of the family to mentally prepare. Of course, he prayed when he got into sticky situations, but he has not had a relationship with God in forever.

The church's expansion was immaculate including the parking lot, and Matt was very impressed. He followed his parents inside, as he did when he was a kid, and he was nervous about the church service. He already felt like a hypocrite being there and was sure he was not going to be open to the sermon or let it change his stony heart. Filing into the church pews beside his siblings, he was happy to see them this morning. He could feel the love coming from their eyes and the excitement they felt because he was there, even if it was for a few moments.

The love in the atmosphere at church is what Matt longed for, and he did not realize he missed it until that very moment. Church felt good to Matt as he enjoyed the singing, the dancing, and the sermon. They reminded him of simpler times in his childhood. With all the fun he had with the family, it was time to return home two months later. Vacation and the visit home were exactly what he needed before he found his next assignment. He decided not to take as much time off between the last engagement and the new one this time so his mind would be occupied with something other than his recent church visit.

Ever since he went to church with his family, his corrupt actions weighed heavily on his mind. He loved this lifestyle too much to give up his wicked ways though. The finer things in life had always been the most attractive, the most comfortable, and the most desired by Matt even when he was a kid. There were many fights between his parents and him when he was growing up. He refused to wear the basic clothing and shoes. Matt always had a side hustle to support his greedy and expensive appetite.

Four weeks later, Matt sat in a conference room surrounded by executives trying to convince them that he was the perfect addition to their team. He detailed his roles as CFO, President, and Executive Director and boasted about his leadership skills. Initially, the interview was proceeding smoothly, and Matt controlled the show. However, a gentleman who oversaw another division, started asking detailed questions, accursedly probing instead of asking for a clearer understanding. There was no way this guy knew Matt was a fraud. They clearly did not run in the same circle. With eight point eight million people living in their city, the guy working for a company that Matt previously scammed was slim to none.

At the end of the interview, the gentlemen approached Matt and asked him if he worked at a Law Firm across town. The guy did not stop his lines of questioning as he reminded Matt money had been embezzled from their clients and the Firm had to shut down completely as their reputation was ruined in the city. They should have done a better job protecting their sensitive information, and this guy was crazy if he assumed Matt was going to fess up to a crime he barely remembered. The guy also told Matt the FBI had never been able to find the thief, as he worked under an alias. One thing Matt could be certain of is if he worked at the Firm, he embezzled as much as he could from them before making his final exit.

Walking away from the inquisitive guy, who ruined this opportunity for Matt to work at the company, he thanked everyone in the room and made a note to disconnect the phone number he used for the interview. Matt was not going to have someone standing over his shoulder questioning him every day, if he accepted the position. Annoyed he had to come up with a new scam, he was still going to figure out a way to rob the company anyway. The guy's division would not see the wrath coming that Matt was getting ready to reign on it. Loving a challenge, he could not wait to get home to devise a plan to destroy this guy's career immediately.

It did not take long for Matt to figure out the guy's region or top clients, thanks to the financial statements. Matt visited each client with a proposal for them to make a lot more money, more aggressively, if they backed his company instead of whoever they currently invested. Many of them were not willing to take their complete business away from their precious firm, but they invested up to forty percent for a stake in Matt's promising new company. After signing a few contracts and receiving wires for down payments, Matt's plan was coming together beautifully. The quarterly financial statements showed a decrease in the guy's division and Matt committed to playing the long game with him for a few more months.

Little to Matt's knowledge, the guy suspected Matt was behind the dropping numbers once he heard a new company in town was stealing his clients. The guy set up a meeting with the new company, with the help of one of his clients, to get to the bottom of things. Knowing this meeting was a little suspicious, as no one ever contacted him first to close a deal, Matt reached out to one of his partners in crime. Matt asked him to attend the meeting for him and report back all the information he could. His partner delivered, as he recorded the interaction with Matt's new nemesis. The negative press from this guy was beginning to infuriate Matt and it was time to destroy him completely. Destroying his career by taking money away from him was not enough.

Matt's enemy lived a very public life, as he liked people to see how likable he was, and shared personal details about his life whenever he had an audience. Finding out where his wife worked and what schools his kids attended, Matt concluded this was going to be like taking candy from a baby. Targeting his wife first, Matt showed up at the gym where she worked out during her lunch breaks. He became the familiar guy at the gym who was willing to show her new techniques to challenge her body.

Eventually, Matt talked her into going for coffee with him. He paid someone to take pictures of them walking from the gym to the coffee shop. As innocent as their conversations were, Matt believed a picture could painted anything you wanted it to be. He did not care the damage he could cause in their marriage, as he posted the pictures on every social media site and tagged both partners. Phase One was complete, and Matt celebrated by going on a ten thousand dollar shopping spree.

Matt remained untouchable and his adversary was not able to find out anything about him or his many aliases. Hiring private investigators, he wanted horrific details to be revealed so Matt could feel pain like he did. Matt kept close to the gossip circuit, and the news fell in his lap that the guy was looking for him. It was time to up the ante and visit his children's school. Involving someone's kids to punish them was a new low for Matt, and his heart twitched. The kids went to various after-school programs, and Matt presented a rock-climbing class so he could get his feet in the door at the kids' school.

The next week, Matt taught the middle schoolers enrolled in his after-school program to rock climb safely. As he connected names to faces, he gathered that his adversary's kids were in his class, as he suspected they would be. Three days later, Matt persuaded the son to tell him personal details about his dad. The little boy disclosed that his dad worked too much, but he and his sister always had the best of everything.

Matt had an unfair contest in class where the winner was chosen before the exercise began, and he would award the winner with a trip to the local ice cream parlor. Of course, his enemy's son won and brought his sister along for the ride. He contacted all the parents of his students in class to tell them class was ending twenty minutes early but his enemy and his wife. As if on cue, an innocent bystander was willing to take pictures of Matt and the guy's kids.

Matt texted his enemy and his wife the pictures with the caption of how easy it was to play this game. Arriving back at school an hour later to a heavy police presence and scared kids at the school, Matt cannot believe he was too sloppy to not have come up with a return plan to drop them off. He was not holding the kids for ransom. He only wanted to send a message to his enemy that accessing everything he loved was easy. He told the kids to enter the gym where their parents would be waiting, and he apologized for losing track of time. Convincing them to go ahead of him, he lied to them that he had to grab trophies out of the car. The kids ran ahead, and Matt left the school as fast as he could.

Racing away from the school, feeling like his mission was complete, Matt could not look at himself in the mirror. He did not know when he became a despicable monster that would take someone's kids to scare them. Just like his other scams, Matt began to pray that God would help him out of his mess, and he vowed never to do it again. He did not stop his car until he was in front of his parents' front door. His dad answered the door after Matt knocked as his life depended on it. Matt told his dad he was in the worst trouble he had ever been in his life, and vengeance had clouded his vision. His mom listened from the hallway and let the men have their private time. She cried at how lost her son's life was. Her worst nightmare was nothing in comparison to the life he lived.

After a good night's sleep and feeling safe at his parent's house, he worked on a new vision and plan for his life. As soon as he could figure out where, Matt was going to start an honest life somewhere far away where he did not have to look over his shoulders. He had the skills, the education, and the elegance to work high-paid legitimate jobs, and this time he planned to do it the honest way. Again, his parents and siblings disbelieved Matt's new plan was all talk until Matt went to church on Sunday and recommitted his life to God. Not only did he talk differently, but he also looked differently when he interacted with his family. For the first time in years, they all rallied behind Matt for moral support. Matt explained to them he carried out some inconceivable things as of late, and they understood his reason for leaving town.

Matt's wife held his hand as his kids stood on the sides of them waiting to be introduced as the newest Pastor at their new church. He was becoming the Pastor in charge of the Prison Reformed Program established years ago at the church. Able to identify with the men's mishaps firsthand, he guaranteed an increased success rate in the failing program. Although he did not serve any time in prison, he committed enough crime to be there for the rest of his life.

Hearing the applauds after his name was called, he squeezed his wife's hand tighter and told the kids to come with them. Seeing his parent's and siblings' faces beaming with pride as soon as he walked into the sanctuary were welcoming. Matt looked to the sky and thanked God for loving him and the redemption he sat aside just for him.

About the Author

Katrina A. McCain grew up in a small town named Nashville, NC where five thousand, five hundred people reside. Having big dreams and bigger goals, Katrina relocated to Greensboro, NC in 2004, where she currently lives. After settling in Greensboro, for a couple of years, Katrina completed her *Bachelor of Science in Accounting* at Guilford College. She currently works as an Accountant at a non-profit agency serving the youth in Guilford County and the surrounding areas.

Katrina formed a "Relay for Life" team affectionately named, "Team McCain." Each year, she and her team raise money for The American Cancer Society to support her own personal battle with cancer and to support others battling cancer too.

As a proud author of her poetry book titled, **Because She Decided to Love**; Katrina has been featured in Poet Speak Magazine, Influential Women Who Win, and Blessings Magazine. Since the release of her first poetry book, she created her own Cross Market Monday Show in which she highlights other small business owners and entrepreneurs. Katrina created an Author Spotlight as another way to give back by providing free reviews on other authors' books she read.

Katrina released her second book, **Then The Unexpected Happened**, in which she self-published, adding another accolade to her list of many. A dedicated member of her family goes without saying; as the Publisher, Author, Poet, Businesswoman, Entrepreneur demonstrate how family comes first in her life while she is busy producing literary works.

Follow Katrina A. McCain

Website: www.iampoetkatrinamccain.com

Facebook: www.facebook.com/poetkatrinamccain

Instagram: www.instagram.com/poetkatrinamccain

Tik Tok: www.tiktok.com/poetkatrinamccain

Twitter: www.twitter.com/McCainPoet

YouTube: Poet Katrina McCain

Other Books

by Katrina A Mccain

Because She Decided to Love:
Poems of Love & Relationships

Then The Unexpected Happened:
A Collection of Poetry

Upcoming Projects

Katrina A. McCain is currently working on a Collection of Poetry. Here is a sneak preview featuring the poem titled, "I Am Lost Without You."

"I Am Lost Without You!"

The truth of the matter is,
I am lost without you!
The volume of your absence,
Echoes loudly when I get lonely.
Always a present thought in my mind,
I cringe from not being able to hold you.
The void of you seems so unendurable
Until I am reminded of your sweet sniffs.
You buried yourself in my neck and chest,
Until I became putty in your arms.
Literally melting from the memories,
I struggle through another day.
I am lost without you!
It gets easier they say,
As everything has gotten harder.
This past year revealed things,
Along with implicit truths.
People are not always kind or honest,

Even when you reveal your broken heart.

I may never find another lover,

Who adores all of me like you did.

I count it a blessing God sent you,

To love me without stipulations or limits.

Still believing in the possibility of love,

I am lost without you!

Made in the USA
Middletown, DE
04 November 2023